In Search of the
INDIAN VILLAGE

Books by Mamang Dai

Fiction
The Black Hill
Escaping the Land
Stupid Cupid
The Legends of Pensam

Poetry
Hambreelmai's Loom
Midsummer Survival Lyrics
The Balm of Time
River Poems

Non-fiction
Mountain Harvest: The Food of Arunachal
Arunachal Pradesh: The Hidden Land

In Search of the
INDIAN VILLAGE
stories & reports

edited by
MAMANG DAI

ALEPH

ALEPH

ALEPH BOOK COMPANY
An independent publishing firm
promoted by *Rupa Publications India.*

First published in India in 2024
by Aleph Book Company
7/16 Ansari Road, Daryaganj
New Delhi 110 002

ISBN: 978-81-19635-78-8

1 3 5 7 9 10 8 6 4 2

Printed in India.

A NOTE ON THE BOOK

In order to preserve the form and flavour of the pieces as they were originally published, the texts have not been standardized according to Aleph's house style. In a couple of pieces, notes, references, and cross-references have been excised.

The soul of India lives in its villages.

—Mahatma Gandhi

CONTENTS

INTRODUCTION

Unforgettable landscape. Unforgettable, the lives of people with their stories of birth, death, life, and longing scattered across the land. I always thought of the village as birthplace, the place tied to our earliest memories. It was from villages that we travelled out to towns and cities. I looked up the definition of village—larger than a hamlet, smaller than a town. It wasn't much to go on, but the name of my hometown popped up on Google Maps. It is tagged as a smart city today, but even so it remains in my mind as a small place, one among the many. According to the 2011 Census, India has around 649,481villages where approximately 68 per cent of its population lives.[1] However, considering the number of unsurveyed villages, forest and revenue villages, uninhabited villages, and so on, the exact count may vary according to the classification of administrative entities defined by different ministries and government databases.

What is certain is that there is a terrain, a place name that is imminent, on the tip of our tongues in every conversation. Unforgettable, that piece of land where many of us were born. The small village many of us left, in search of new territory— some to return, some to never come back. In the words of Mahatma Gandhi: 'If the village perishes India will perish too.'

What then, is an Indian village? Why does it matter, so much so that in order not to perish a country must ensure its survival?

It is what this book is about. Turn the pages, and the reader will find a view of the village presented in all its immensity. Small village—big meaning. Life pristine as the images in Ruskin Bond's 'The Blue Umbrella', floating close to the sky, soft as a breeze unfurling in a coming-of-age story, a magic moment of sharing when a small umbrella belongs to both the young owner and the old villager who covets it. People say village life is the simple life. It is close to nature, away from the fumes and pollution of the city. Holidaymakers arrive from the plains to picnic in forest glades, but not all villages are the same. There are big villages, rich villages, and others with less than a hundred households. Many villages are poor, abandoned in the mountaintops, others are burgeoning tourist destinations. There are villages of landowners, jotedars, and mahajans; the terror and misery of another land that is a killing field soaked in blood where corpses lie buried like seed, in Mahasweta Devi's 'Seed'. Every day a man sits watch over a stony field. Every night he spreads his mat and goes to sleep. The barren strip of land holds unspeakable secrets. He who opens his mouth will die. When the storm breaks, intense as the flames of an ancient fire, the corpses buried in the heart rise up—*to be a seed is to stay alive.*

Apart from language, population, and religious demographics, Indian villages also have their regional diversity and differ from one another in distinct, definable ways. The stereotypical villager is unschooled, poor; its population only good at field work. Village life is a precarious hand-to-mouth existence, yet far from the noise of urban life there is a dignity and quietude in the daily lives of men and women living in these villages. 'Coinsanv's Cattle' by Damodar Mauzo is a hauntingly nuanced portrayal of love and sacrifice in the face of hardship. Home is where the heart is. Despite the worries about seedlings, fertilizer, weeding, the need for cash, men and women live like the fruit and flowers around them, and the animals that they keep are their own kin.

In Vijaydan Detha's 'Countless Hitlers', the men are farmers who looked as if they had been born of the earth's womb, as if they had grown up and blossomed among the kareel, aak, khejari, and acacia trees. Yet as in all human settlements human nature takes over—the will to do good struggling with hunger, envy, and covetousness, mobilized by new money that leaves a trail of blood on the Ajmer–Jodhpur Road. A brand new, blood-red tractor has crushed an innocent cyclist in a fit of rivalry. 'Brain-white smudges on a blood-red background. Shards of broken glass. A man's dead body. White shorts. Bloodied sky-blue undershirt. Mashed dreams. Streams of love. The painting wasn't bad!' writes Detha, considering it was done by a band of rustics.

'What is a village but a sink of localism, a den of ignorance, narrow mindedness and communalism?' This was B. R. Ambedkar's vehement critique of the social structure of the village and caste. Ambedkar knew first-hand that the ideal of a model village as outlined by Gandhi in 'My Idea of Village Swaraj' was a far cry from the reality of Indian village life. In *The Indian Village: Rural Lives in the 21st Century*, Surinder S. Jodhka offers scholarly insight into the concept of village and village-ism. There is Gandhi arguing for the village as the site of 'India's soul', there is Nehru the modernist with his vision of social transformation, and B. R. Ambedkar, the anti-village advocate calling for radical transformation of village communities. It's another picture—a landscape of villages like a far-off country slowly emerges. Who dwells there? What is a man thinking about? Who is that woman by the well? Are the children happy? There are opposing views and prescriptions for the future of India's villages and rural development, yet the thing itself, the Indian village, seems to defy our imagination about their future.

In a telling line P. Sainath wrote: 'In a selfish sense, rural India is a journalist's paradise.' The cast of characters is as rich and varied as the country. Sainath introduces the reader to a host of quirky heroes, despots, distillers, poets, and artists, tracing a rejuvenating journey through the length and breadth of the country right up to where we meet Ponnusamy, the writer and the village, in far Melanmarai Nadu, a place so difficult to find that he, Sainath, arrived six hours late for their appointment.

The joys of travelling through the countryside are real. 'Joy is less common, no doubt, but is as real as suffering,' quotes Amitava Kumar in his short biography of Patna, *A Matter of Rats*. Ostensibly a story about the ubiquitous rat inhabiting every conceivable place in the city this is also about rat catchers and food, and how what we eat, or not, is a marker of caste. Yet the highway to progress is ever expanding, and the old village that the author had returned to visit 'was now but a stone's throw from the world of TV broadcasting and even beauty parlours'.

In colonial times India was the land of villages that had remained unchanged for centuries. Today rural life is changed or absorbed into expanding cities as populations migrate for economic or social reasons. In population demographics count, 37.8 per cent of India's total population are migrants, in search of work, a new life.[2] Other than highways and man-made constructions there are other forces at work. In coastal Andhra it is the sea that is rearranging the shoreline. In 'Oh, That House? It's in the Sea Now—There!', Rahul M depicts Uppada, East Godavari District, where everyone has moved house at one time or another to escape the sea. And like the sea chipping away at these villages some of the customs and practices associated with the caste system began to weaken as the more affluent moved further away from the sea, says Rahul. In a way the sea has liberated social groups categorized as backward classes in a settled community, into a new freedom.

In time, much of what we remember is changed. There are villages, temples, and mosques buried in the earth or drowned, under the waters. As the roofs of houses disappear a vision of a window frame, a familiar outline of a riverbank, a path of shade trees begins to take shape. There is a man walking alone on a footpath. He wades into a river overwhelmed with memories and once he has crossed the river, he sinks down to the riverbank and weeps. O. V. Vijayan's story 'The Hanging' winds itself like a noose around our necks. A father is travelling to Kannur to witness his son's execution. Who can say anything about fathers and sons, about crime and punishment? Words are inadequate to describe the weight of sorrow, the torrent of unsaid things. Everywhere people live with hopes and fears. Lives matter. Death comes, and in villages and cities, small-town people gather their memories into a tight bundle and scatter what little offering they have, to the wind, to the quiet sea, like the grains of sacrificial rice in O. V. Vijayan's story, under the 'gleaming sunlit dome of the sky'.

Villages, villagers, village life. A mapping of new settlements with roads and buildings. Where will these roads lead, for the nation's villages? Perhaps the reader will find a new perspective on the evolving realities of rural life in the significant reports and stories presented here. Villages and cities grow side by side. And sometimes, where the lines merge in these contested territories, another horizon appears.

Mamang Dai
Pasighat
December 2023

FICTION

THE BLUE UMBRELLA

Ruskin Bond

I

'Neelu! Neelu!' cried Binya.

She scrambled barefoot over the rocks, ran over the short summer grass, up and over the brow of the hill, all the time calling 'Neelu, Neelu!' Neelu—Blue—was the name of the blue-grey cow. The other cow, which was white, was called Gori, meaning Fair One. They were fond of wandering off on their own, down to the stream or into the pine forest, and sometimes they came back by themselves and sometimes they stayed away—almost deliberately, it seemed to Binya.

If the cows didn't come home at the right time, Binya would be sent to fetch them. Sometimes her brother, Bijju, went with her, but these days he was busy preparing for his exams and didn't have time to help with the cows.

Binya liked being on her own, and sometimes she allowed the cows to lead her into some distant valley, and then they would all be late coming home. The cows preferred having Binya with them, because she let them wander. Bijju pulled them by their tails if they went too far.

Binya belonged to the mountains, to this part of the Himalaya known as Garhwal. Dark forests and lonely hilltops held no terrors for her. It was only when she was in the market town, jostled by the crowds in the bazaar, that she felt rather nervous and lost. The town, five miles from the village, was also a pleasure resort for tourists from all over India.

Binya was probably ten. She may have been nine or even eleven, she couldn't be sure because no one in the village kept birthdays; but her mother told her she'd been born during a winter when the snow had come up to the windows, and that was just over ten years ago, wasn't it? Two years later, her father had died, but his passing had made no difference to their way of life. They had three tiny terraced fields on the side of the mountain, and they grew potatoes, onions, ginger, beans, mustard, and maize: not enough to sell in the town, but enough to live on.

Like most mountain girls, Binya was quite sturdy, fair of skin, with pink cheeks and dark eyes, and her black hair tied in a pigtail. She wore pretty glass bangles on her wrists, and a necklace of glass beads. From the necklace hung a leopard's claw. It was a lucky charm, and Binya always wore it. Bijju had one, too, only his was attached to a string.

Binya's full name was Binyadevi, and Bijju's real name was Vijay, but everyone called them Binya and Bijju. Binya was two years younger than her brother.

She had stopped calling for Neelu; she had heard the cowbells tinkling, and knew the cows hadn't gone far. Singing to herself, she walked over fallen pine needles into the forest glade on the spur of the hill. She heard voices, laughter, the clatter of plates and cups, and stepping through the trees, she came upon a party of picnickers.

They were holidaymakers from the plains. The women were dressed in bright saris, the men wore light summer shirts, and the children had pretty new clothes. Binya, standing in the shadows between the trees, went unnoticed; for some time she watched the picnickers, admiring their clothes, listening to their unfamiliar accents, and gazing rather hungrily at the sight of all their food. And then her gaze came to rest on a bright blue umbrella, a frilly thing for women, which lay open on the grass beside its owner.

Now Binya had seen umbrellas before, and her mother had a big black umbrella which nobody used any more because the field rats had eaten holes in it, but this was the first time Binya had seen such a small, dainty, colourful umbrella, and she fell in love with it. The umbrella was like a flower, a great blue flower that had sprung up on the dry brown hillside.

She moved forward a few paces so that she could see the umbrella better. As she came out of the shadows into the sunlight, the picnickers saw her.

'Hello, look who's here!' exclaimed the older of the two women. 'A little village girl!'

'Isn't she pretty?' remarked the other. 'But how torn and dirty her clothes are!' It did not seem to bother them that Binya could hear and understand everything they said about her.

'They're very poor in the hills,' said one of the men.

'Then let's give her something to eat.' And the older woman beckoned to Binya to come closer.

Hesitantly, nervously, Binya approached the group.

Normally she would have turned and fled, but the attraction was the pretty blue umbrella. It had cast a spell over her, drawing her forward almost against her will.

'What's that on her neck?' asked the younger woman.

'A necklace of sorts.'

'It's a pendant—see, there's a claw hanging from it!'

'It's a tiger's claw,' said the man beside her. (He had never seen a tiger's claw.) 'A lucky charm. These people wear them to keep away evil spirits.' He looked to Binya for confirmation, but Binya said nothing.

'Oh, I want one too!' said the woman, who was obviously his wife.

'You can't get them in shops.'

'Buy hers, then. Give her two or three rupees, she's sure to need the money.'

The man, looking slightly embarrassed but anxious to please his young wife, produced a two-rupee note and offered it to Binya, indicating that he wanted the pendant in exchange. Binya put her hand to the necklace, half afraid that the excited woman would snatch it away from her. Solemnly she shook her head.

The man then showed her a five-rupee note, but again Binya shook her head.

'How silly she is!' exclaimed the young woman.

'It may not be hers to sell,' said the man. 'But I'll try again. How much do you want—what can we give you?' And he waved his hand towards the picnic things scattered about on the grass.

Without any hesitation Binya pointed to the umbrella.

'My umbrella!' exclaimed the young woman. 'She wants my umbrella. What cheek!'

'Well, you want her pendant, don't you?'

'That's different.'

'Is it?'

The man and his wife were beginning to quarrel with each other.

'I'll ask her to go away,' said the older woman. 'We're making such fools of ourselves.'

'But I want the pendant!' cried the other, petulantly.

And then, on an impulse, she picked up the umbrella and held it out to Binya.

'Here, take the umbrella!'

Binya removed her necklace and held it out to the young woman, who immediately placed it around her own neck. Then Binya took the umbrella and held it up. It did not look so small in her hands; in fact, it was just the right size.

She had forgotten about the picnickers, who were busy examining the pendant. She turned the blue umbrella this way and that, looked through the bright blue silk at the pulsating sun, and then, still keeping it open, turned and disappeared into the forest glade.

II

Binya seldom closed the blue umbrella. Even when she had it in the house, she left it lying open in a corner of the room. Sometimes Bijju snapped it shut, complaining that it got in the way. She would open it again a little later. It wasn't beautiful when it was closed.

Whenever Binya went out—whether it was to graze the cows, or fetch water from the spring, or carry milk to the little tea shop on the Tehri road—she took the umbrella with her. That patch of sky-blue silk could always be seen on the hillside.

Old Ram Bharosa (Ram the Trustworthy) kept the tea shop on the Tehri road. It was a dusty, unmetalled road. Once a day, the Tehri bus stopped near his shop and passengers got down to sip hot tea or drink a glass of curd. He kept a few bottles of Coca-Cola too, but as there was no ice, the bottles got hot in the sun and so were seldom opened. He also kept sweets and toffees, and when Binya or Bijju had a few coins to spare, they would spend them at the shop. It was only a mile from the village.

Ram Bharosa was astonished to see Binya's blue umbrella.

'What have you there, Binya?' he asked.

Binya gave the umbrella a twirl and smiled at Ram Bharosa. She was always ready with her smile, and would willingly have lent it to anyone who was feeling unhappy.

'That's a lady's umbrella,' said Ram Bharosa. 'That's only for memsahibs. Where did you get it?'

'Someone gave it to me—for my necklace.'

'You exchanged it for your lucky claw!'

Binya nodded.

'But what do you need it for? The sun isn't hot enough, and it isn't meant for the rain. It's just a pretty thing for rich ladies to play with!'

Binya nodded and smiled again. Ram Bharosa was quite right; it was just a beautiful plaything. And that was exactly why she had fallen in love with it.

'I have an idea,' said the shopkeeper. 'It's no use to you, that umbrella. Why not sell it to me? I'll give you five rupees for it.'

'It's worth fifteen,' said Binya.

'Well, then, I'll give you ten.'

Binya laughed and shook her head.

'Twelve rupees?' said Ram Bharosa, but without much hope.

Binya placed a five-paise coin on the counter.

'I came for a toffee,' she said.

Ram Bharosa pulled at his drooping whiskers, gave Binya a wry look, and placed a toffee in the palm of her hand. He watched Binya as she walked away along the dusty road. The blue umbrella held him fascinated, and he stared after it until it was out of sight.

The villagers used this road to go to the market town. Some used the bus, a few rode on mules, and most people walked. Today, everyone on the road turned their heads to stare at the girl with the bright blue umbrella.

Binya sat down in the shade of a pine tree. The umbrella, still open, lay beside her. She cradled her head in her arms, and presently she dozed off. It was that kind of day, sleepily warm and summery.

And while she slept, a wind sprang up.

It came quietly, swishing gently through the trees, humming softly. Then it was joined by other random gusts, bustling over the tops of the mountains. The trees shook their heads and came to life. The wind fanned Binya's cheeks. The umbrella stirred on the grass.

The wind grew stronger, picking up dead leaves and sending them spinning and swirling through the air. It got into the umbrella and began to drag it over the grass. Suddenly it lifted the umbrella and carried it about six feet from the sleeping girl. The sound woke Binya.

She was on her feet immediately, and then she was

leaping down the steep slope. But just as she was within reach of the umbrella, the wind picked it up again and carried it further downhill.

Binya set off in pursuit. The wind was in a wicked, playful mood. It would leave the umbrella alone for a few moments, but as soon as Binya came near, it would pick up the umbrella again and send it bouncing, floating, dancing away from her.

The hill grew steeper. Binya knew that after twenty yards it would fall away in a precipice. She ran faster. And the wind ran with her, ahead of her, and the blue umbrella stayed up with the wind.

A fresh gust picked it up and carried it to the very edge of the cliff. There it balanced for a few seconds, before toppling over, out of sight.

Binya ran to the edge of the cliff. Going down on her hands and knees, she peered down the cliff face. About a hundred feet below, a small stream rushed between great boulders. Hardly anything grew on the cliff face—just a few stunted bushes, and, halfway down, a wild cherry tree growing crookedly out of the rocks and hanging across the chasm. The umbrella had stuck in the cherry tree.

Binya didn't hesitate. She may have been timid with strangers, but she was at home on a hillside. She stuck her bare leg over the edge of the cliff and began climbing down. She kept her face to the hillside, feeling her way with her feet, only changing her handhold when she knew her feet were secure. Sometimes she held on to the thorny bilberry bushes, but she did not trust the other plants, which came away very easily.

Loose stones rattled down the cliff. Once on their way,

the stones did not stop until they reached the bottom of the hill; and they took other stones with them, so that there was soon a cascade of stones, and Binya had to be very careful not to start a landslide.

As agile as a mountain goat, she did not take more than five minutes to reach the crooked cherry tree. But the most difficult task remained—she had to crawl along the trunk of the tree, which stood out at right angles from the cliff. Only by doing this could she reach the trapped umbrella.

Binya felt no fear when climbing trees. She was proud of the fact that she could climb them as well as Bijju. Gripping the rough cherry bark with her toes, and using her knees as leverage, she crawled along the trunk of the projecting tree until she was almost within reach of the umbrella. She noticed with dismay that the blue cloth was torn in a couple of places.

She looked down, and it was only then that she felt afraid. She was right over the chasm, balanced precariously about eighty feet above the boulder-strewn stream. Looking down, she felt quite dizzy. Her hands shook, and the tree shook too. If she slipped now, there was only one direction in which she could fall—down, down, into the depths of that dark and shadowy ravine.

There was only one thing to do; concentrate on the patch of blue just a couple of feet away from her. She did not look down or up, but straight ahead, and willing herself forward, she managed to reach the umbrella.

She could not crawl back with it in her hands. So, after dislodging it from the forked branch in which it had stuck, she let it fall, still open, into the ravine below.

Cushioned by the wind, the umbrella floated serenely downwards, landing in a thicket of nettles.

Binya crawled back along the trunk of the cherry tree. Twenty minutes later, she emerged from the nettle clump, her precious umbrella held aloft. She had nettle stings all over her legs, but she was hardly aware of the smarting. She was as immune to nettles as Bijju was to bees.

III

About four years previously, Bijju had knocked a hive out of an oak tree, and had been badly stung on the face and legs. It had been a painful experience. But now, if a bee stung him, he felt nothing at all: he had been immunized for life!

He was on his way home from school. It was two o'clock and he hadn't eaten since six in the morning. Fortunately, the kingora bushes—the bilberries—were in fruit, and already Bijju's lips were stained purple with the juice of the wild, sour fruit.

He didn't have any money to spend at Ram Bharosa's shop, but he stopped there anyway to look at the sweets in their glass jars.

'And what will you have today?' asked Ram Bharosa.

'No money,' said Bijju.

'You can pay me later.'

Bijju shook his head. Some of his friends had taken sweets on credit, and at the end of the month they had found they'd eaten more sweets than they could possibly pay for! As a result, they'd had to hand over to Ram Bharosa some of their most treasured possessions—such as a curved knife for cutting grass, or a small hand-axe, or a jar for pickles, or a pair of earrings—and these had become the shopkeeper's possessions and were kept by him or sold in his shop.

Ram Bharosa had set his heart on having Binya's blue umbrella, and so naturally he was anxious to give credit to either of the children, but so far neither had fallen into the trap.

Bijju moved on, his mouth full of kingora berries. Halfway home, he saw Binya with the cows. It was late evening, and the sun had gone down, but Binya still had the umbrella open. The two small rents had been stitched up by her mother.

Bijju gave his sister a handful of berries. She handed him the umbrella while she ate the berries.

'You can have the umbrella until we get home,' she said. It was her way of rewarding Bijju for bringing her the wild fruit.

Calling 'Neelu! Gori!' Binya and Bijju set out for home, followed at some distance by the cows.

It was dark before they reached the village, but Bijju still had the umbrella open.

Most of the people in the village were a little envious of Binya's blue umbrella. No one else had ever possessed one like it. The schoolmaster's wife thought it was quite wrong for a poor cultivator's daughter to have such a fine umbrella while she, a second class BA, had to make do with an ordinary black one. Her husband offered to have their old umbrella dyed blue; she gave him a scornful look, and loved him a little less than before. The pujari, who looked after the temple, announced that he would buy a multi-coloured umbrella the next time he was in the town. A few days later he returned looking annoyed and grumbling that they weren't available except in Delhi. Most people consoled themselves by saying that Binya's pretty umbrella wouldn't keep out the rain, if it rained heavily; that it would shrivel in the sun, if the sun was fierce; that it would collapse in a wind, if the wind was strong; that it would attract lightning, if lightning fell near it; and that it would prove unlucky, if there was any ill luck going about. Secretly, everyone admired it.

Unlike the adults, the children didn't have to pretend. They were full of praise for the umbrella. It was so light, so pretty, so bright a blue! And it was just the right size for Binya. They knew that if they said nice things about the umbrella, Binya would smile and give it to them to hold for a little while—just a very little while!

Soon it was the time of the monsoon. Big black clouds kept piling up, and thunder rolled over the hills.

Binya sat on the hillside all afternoon, waiting for the rain. As soon as the first big drop of rain came down, she raised the umbrella over her head. More drops, big ones, came pattering down. She could see them through the umbrella silk as they broke against the cloth.

And then there was a cloudburst, and it was like standing under a waterfall. The umbrella wasn't really a rain umbrella, but it held up bravely. Only Binya's feet got wet. Rods of rain fell around her in a curtain of shivered glass.

Everywhere on the hillside people were scurrying for shelter. Some made for a charcoal burner's hut, others for a mule shed, or Ram Bharosa's shop. Binya was the only one who didn't run. This was what she'd been waiting for—rain on her umbrella—and she wasn't in a hurry to go home. She didn't mind getting her feet wet. The cows didn't mind getting wet either.

Presently she found Bijju sheltering in a cave. He would have enjoyed getting wet, but he had his schoolbooks with him and he couldn't afford to let them get spoilt. When he saw Binya, he came out of the cave and shared the umbrella. He was a head taller than his sister, so he had to hold the umbrella for her, while she held his books.

The cows had been left far behind.

'Neelu, Neelu!' called Binya.

'Gori!' called Bijju.

When their mother saw them sauntering home through the driving rain, she called out: 'Binya! Bijju! Hurry up, and bring the cows in! What are you doing out there in the rain?'

'Just testing the umbrella,' said Bijju.

IV

The rains set in, and the sun only made brief appearances. The hills turned a lush green. Ferns sprang up on walls and tree trunks. Giant lilies reared up like leopards from the tall grass. A white mist coiled and uncoiled as it floated up from the valley. It was a beautiful season, except for the leeches.

Every day, Binya came home with a couple of leeches fastened to the flesh of her bare legs. They fell off by themselves just as soon as they'd had their thimbleful of blood, but you didn't know they were on you until they fell off, and then, later, the skin became very sore and itchy. Some of the older people still believed that to be bled by leeches was a remedy for various ailments. Whenever Ram Bharosa had a headache, he applied a leech to his throbbing temple.

Three days of incessant rain had flooded out a number of small animals who lived in holes in the ground. Binya's mother suddenly found the roof full of field rats. She had to drive them out; they ate too much of her stored-up wheat flour and rice. Bijju liked lifting up large rocks to disturb the scorpions who were sleeping beneath. And snakes came out to bask in the sun.

Binya had just crossed the small stream at the bottom of the hill when she saw something gliding out of the bushes and coming towards her. It was a long black snake. A clatter of loose stones frightened it. Seeing the girl in its way, it rose up, hissing, prepared to strike. The forked tongue darted out, the venomous head lunged at Binya.

Binya's umbrella was open as usual. She thrust it forward, between herself and the snake, and the snake's hard snout thudded twice against the strong silk of the umbrella. The reptile then turned and slithered away over the wet rocks, disappearing into a clump of ferns.

Binya forgot about the cows and ran all the way home to tell her mother how she had been saved by the umbrella. Bijju had to put away his books and go out to fetch the cows. He carried a stout stick, in case he met with any snakes.

First the summer sun, and now the endless rain, meant that the umbrella was beginning to fade a little. From a bright blue it had changed to a light blue. But it was still a pretty thing, and tougher than it looked, and Ram Bharosa still desired it. He did not want to sell it; he wanted to own it. He was probably the richest man in the area—so why shouldn't he have a blue umbrella? Not a day passed without his getting a glimpse of Binya and the umbrella; and the more he saw the umbrella, the more he wanted it.

The schools closed during the monsoon, but this didn't

mean that Bijju could sit at home doing nothing. Neelu and Gori were providing more milk than was required at home, so Binya's mother was able to sell a kilo of milk every day: half a kilo to the schoolmaster, and half a kilo (at reduced rate) to the temple pujari. Bijju had to deliver the milk every morning.

Ram Bharosa had asked Bijju to work in his shop during the holidays, but Bijju didn't have time—he had to help his mother with the ploughing and the transplanting of the rice seedlings. So Ram Bharosa employed a boy from the next village, a boy called Rajaram. He did all the washing-up and ran various errands. He went to the same school as Bijju, but the two boys were not friends.

One day, as Binya passed the shop, twirling her blue umbrella, Rajaram noticed that his employer gave a deep sigh and began muttering to himself.

'What's the matter, babuji?' asked the boy.

'Oh, nothing,' said Ram Bharosa. 'It's just a sickness that has come upon me. And it's all due to that girl Binya and her wretched umbrella.'

'Why, what has she done to you?'

'Refused to sell me her umbrella! There's pride for you. And I offered her ten rupees.'

'Perhaps, if you gave her twelve....'

'But it isn't new any longer. It isn't worth eight rupees now. All the same, I'd like to have it.'

'You wouldn't make a profit on it,' said Rajaram.

'It's not the profit I'm after, wretch! It's the thing itself. It's the beauty of it!'

'And what would you do with it, babuji? You don't visit

anyone—you're seldom out of your shop. Of what use would it be to you?'

'Of what use is a poppy in a cornfield? Of what use is a rainbow? Of what use are you, numbskull? Wretch! I, too, have a soul. I want the umbrella, because—because I want its beauty to be mine!'

Rajaram put the kettle on to boil, began dusting the counter, all the time muttering: 'I'm as useful as an umbrella,' and then, after a short period of intense thought, said: 'What will you give me, babuji, if I get the umbrella for you?'

'What do you mean?' asked the old man.

'You know what I mean. What will you give me?'

'You mean to steal it, don't you, you wretch? What a delightful child you are! I'm glad you're not my son or my enemy. But look, everyone will know it has been stolen, and then how will I be able to show off with it?'

'You will have to gaze upon it in secret,' said Rajaram with a chuckle. 'Or take it into Tehri, and have it coloured red! That's your problem. But tell me, babuji, do you want it badly enough to pay me three rupees for stealing it without being seen?'

Ram Bharosa gave the boy a long, sad look. 'You're a sharp boy,' he said. 'You'll come to a bad end. I'll give you two rupees.'

'Three,' said the boy.

'Two,' said the old man.

'You don't really want it, I can see that,' said the boy.

'Wretch!' said the old man. 'Evil one! Darkener of my doorstep! Fetch me the umbrella, and I'll give you three rupees.'

V

Binya was in the forest glade where she had first seen the umbrella. No one came there for picnics during the monsoon. The grass was always wet and the pine needles were slippery underfoot. The tall trees shut out the light, and poisonous-looking mushrooms, orange and purple, sprang up everywhere. But it was a good place for porcupines, who seemed to like the mushrooms, and Binya was searching for porcupine quills.

The hill people didn't think much of porcupine quills, but far away in southern India, the quills were valued as charms and sold at a rupee each. So Ram Bharosa paid a tenth of a rupee for each quill brought to him, and he in turn sold the quills at a profit to a trader from the plains.

Binya had already found five quills, and she knew there'd be more in the long grass. For once, she'd put her umbrella down. She had to put it aside if she was to search the ground thoroughly.

It was Rajaram's chance.

He'd been following Binya for some time, concealing himself behind trees and rocks, creeping closer whenever she became absorbed in her search. He was anxious that she should not see him and be able to recognize him later.

He waited until Binya had wandered some distance from the umbrella. Then, running forward at a crouch, he seized the open umbrella and dashed off with it.

But Rajaram had very big feet. Binya heard his heavy footsteps and turned just in time to see him as he disappeared between the trees. She cried out, dropped the porcupine quills, and gave chase.

Binya was swift and sure-footed, but Rajaram had a long stride. All the same, he made the mistake of running downhill. A long-legged person is much faster going uphill than down. Binya reached the edge of the forest glade in time to see the thief scrambling down the path to the stream. He had closed the umbrella so that it would not hinder his flight.

Binya was beginning to gain on the boy. He kept to the path, while she simply slid and leapt down the steep hillside. Near the bottom of the hill the path began to straighten out, and it was here that the long-legged boy began to forge ahead again.

Bijju was coming home from another direction. He had a bundle of sticks which he'd collected for the kitchen fire. As he reached the path, he saw Binya rushing down the hill as though all the mountain spirits in Garhwal were after her.

'What's wrong?' he called. 'Why are you running?'

Binya paused only to point at the fleeing Rajaram.

'My umbrella!' she cried. 'He has stolen it!'

Bijju dropped his bundle of sticks and ran after his sister. When he reached her side, he said, 'I'll soon catch him!' and went sprinting away over the lush green grass. He was fresh, and he was soon well ahead of Binya and gaining on the thief.

Rajaram was crossing the shallow stream when Bijju caught up with him. Rajaram was the taller boy, but Bijju was much stronger. He flung himself at the thief, caught him by the legs, and brought him down in the water. Rajaram got to his feet and tried to drag himself away, but Bijju still had him by a leg. Rajaram overbalanced and came down with a great splash. He had let the umbrella fall. It began to float away on the current. Just then Binya arrived, flushed and breathless, and went dashing into the stream after the umbrella.

Meanwhile, a tremendous fight was taking place. Locked in fierce combat, the two boys swayed together on a rock, tumbled on to the sand, rolled over and over the pebbled bank until they were again thrashing about in the shallows of the stream. The magpies, bulbuls, and other birds were disturbed and flew away with cries of alarm.

Covered with mud, gasping and spluttering, the boys groped for each other in the water. After five minutes of frenzied struggle, Bijju emerged victorious.

Rajaram lay flat on his back on the sand, exhausted, while Bijju sat astride him, pinning him down with his arms and legs.

'Let me get up!' gasped Rajaram. 'Let me go—I don't want your useless umbrella!'

'Then why did you take it?' demanded Bijju. 'Come on—tell me why!'

'It was that skinflint Ram Bharosa,' said Rajaram. 'He told me to get it for him. He said if I didn't fetch it, I'd lose my job.'

VI

By early October, the rains were coming to an end. The leeches disappeared. The ferns turned yellow, and the sunlight on the green hills was mellow and golden, like the limes on the small tree in front of Binya's home. Bijju's days were happy ones as he came home from school, munching on roasted corn. Binya's umbrella had turned a pale milky blue, and was patched in several places, but it was still the

21

prettiest umbrella in the village, and she still carried it with her wherever she went.

The cold, cruel winter wasn't far off, but somehow October seems longer than other months, because it is a kind month: the grass is good to be upon, the breeze is warm and gentle and pine-scented. That October, everyone seemed contented—everyone, that is, except Ram Bharosa.

The old man had by now given up all hope of ever possessing Binya's umbrella. He wished he had never set eyes on it. Because of the umbrella, he had suffered the tortures of greed, the despair of loneliness. Because of the umbrella, people had stopped coming to his shop!

Ever since it had become known that Ram Bharosa had tried to have the umbrella stolen, the village people had turned against him. They stopped trusting the old man, instead of buying their soap and tea and matches from his shop, they preferred to walk an extra mile to the shops near the Tehri bus stand. Who would have dealings with a man who had sold his soul for an umbrella? The children taunted him, twisted his name around. From 'Ram the Trustworthy' he became 'Trusty Umbrella Thief'.

The old man sat alone in his empty shop, listening to the eternal hissing of his kettle and wondering if anyone would ever again step in for a glass of tea. Ram Bharosa had lost his own appetite, and ate and drank very little. There was no money coming in. He had his savings in a bank in Tehri, but it was a terrible thing to have to dip into them! To save money, he had dismissed the blundering Rajaram. So he was left without any company. The roof leaked and the wind got in through the corrugated tin sheets, but Ram Bharosa didn't care.

Bijju and Binya passed his shop almost every day. Bijju went by with a loud but tuneless whistle. He was one of the world's whistlers; cares rested lightly on his shoulders. But, strangely enough, Binya crept quietly past the shop, looking the other way, almost as though she was in some way responsible for the misery of Ram Bharosa.

She kept reasoning with herself, telling herself that the umbrella was her very own, and that she couldn't help it if others were jealous of it. But had she loved the umbrella too much? Had it mattered more to her than people mattered? She couldn't help feeling that, in a small way, she was the cause of the sad look on Ram Bharosa's face ('His face is a yard long,' said Bijju) and the ruinous condition of his shop. It was all due to his own greed, no doubt, but she didn't want him to feel too bad about what he'd done, because it made her feel bad about herself; and so she closed the umbrella whenever she came near the shop, opening it again only when she was out of sight.

One day towards the end of October, when she had ten paise in her pocket, she entered the shop and asked the old man for a toffee.

She was Ram Bharosa's first customer in almost two weeks. He looked suspiciously at the girl. Had she come to taunt him, to flaunt the umbrella in his face? She had placed her coin on the counter. Perhaps it was a bad coin. Ram Bharosa picked it up and bit it; he held it up to the light; he rang it on the ground. It was a good coin. He gave Binya the toffee.

Binya had already left the shop when Ram Bharosa saw the closed umbrella lying on his counter. There it was, the blue umbrella he had always wanted, within his grasp at last! He had only to hide it at the back of his shop, and no one would know that he had it, no one could prove that Binya had left it behind.

He stretched out his trembling, bony hand, and took the umbrella by the handle. He pressed it open. He stood beneath it, in the dark shadows of his shop, where no sun or rain could ever touch it.

'But I'm never in the sun or in the rain,' he said aloud. 'Of what use is an umbrella to me?'

And he hurried outside and ran after Binya.

'Binya, Binya!' he shouted. 'Binya, you've left your umbrella behind!'

He wasn't used to running, but he caught up with her, held out the umbrella, saying, 'You forgot it—the umbrella!'

In that moment it belonged to both of them.

But Binya didn't take the umbrella. She shook her head and said, 'You keep it. I don't need it any more.'

'But it's such a pretty umbrella!' protested Ram Bharosa. 'It's the best umbrella in the village.'

'I know,' said Binya. 'But an umbrella isn't everything.'

And she left the old man holding the umbrella, and went tripping down the road, and there was nothing between her and the bright blue sky.

VII

Well, now that Ram Bharosa has the blue umbrella—a gift from Binya, as he tells everyone—he is sometimes persuaded to go out into the sun or the rain, and as a result he looks much healthier. Sometimes he uses the umbrella to chase away pigs or goats. It is always left open outside the shop, and anyone who wants to borrow it may do so; and so in a way it has become everyone's umbrella. It is faded and patchy, but it is still the best umbrella in the village.

People are visiting Ram Bharosa's shop again. Whenever Bijju or Binya stop for a cup of tea, he gives them a little extra milk or sugar. They like their tea sweet and milky.

A few nights ago, a bear visited Ram Bharosa's shop. There had been snow on the higher ranges of the Himalaya, and the bear had been finding it difficult to obtain food; so it had come lower down, to see what it could pick up near the village. That night it scrambled on to the tin roof of Ram Bharosa's shop, and made off with a huge pumpkin which had been ripening on the roof. But in climbing off the roof, the bear had lost a claw.

Next morning Ram Bharosa found the claw just outside the door of his shop. He picked it up and put it in his pocket. A bear's claw was a lucky find.

A day later, when he went into the market town, he took the claw with him, and left it with a silversmith, giving the craftsman certain instructions. The silversmith made a locket for the claw, then he gave it a thin silver chain. When Ram Bharosa came again, he paid the silversmith ten rupees for his work.

The days were growing shorter, and Binya had to be home a little earlier every evening. There was a hungry leopard at large, and she couldn't leave the cows out after dark.

She was hurrying past Ram Bharosa's shop when the old man called out to her.

'Binya, spare a minute! I want to show you something.'

Binya stepped into the shop.

'What do you think of it?' asked Ram Bharosa, showing her the silver pendant with the claw.

'It's so beautiful,' said Binya, just touching the claw and the silver chain.

'It's a bear's claw,' said Ram Bharosa. 'That's even luckier than a leopard's claw. Would you like to have it?'

'I have no money,' said Binya.

'That doesn't matter. You gave me the umbrella, I give you the claw! Come, let's see what it looks like on you.'

He placed the pendant on Binya, and indeed it looked very beautiful on her.

Ram Bharosa says he will never forget the smile she gave him when she left the shop.

She was halfway home when she realized she had left the cows behind.

'Neelu, Neelu!' she called. 'Oh, Gori!'

There was a faint tinkle of bells as the cows came slowly down the mountain path.

In the distance she could hear her mother and Bijju calling for her.

She began to sing. They heard her singing, and knew she was safe and near.

She walked home through the darkening glade, singing of the stars, and the trees stood still and listened to her, and the mountains were glad.

COUNTLESS HITLERS

Vijaydan Detha

TRANSLATED FROM THE RAJASTHANI
BY CHRISTI A. MERRILL AND KAILASH KABIR

The five were only men. Some younger, some older, all between thirty and fifty. The eldest was beginning to grey here and there, but the others had heads of hair as black as bumblebees. They looked like men: eyes where eyes should be, noses where noses should be, teeth where teeth should be. Arms and legs where arms and legs should be. Copper-coloured complexions. White turbans, some old, some new. Cholas of white muslin, like their dhotis. Knotted gold earrings in their ears. Gold pendants around their necks hung from black cords. Each man spoke like a man. Each man walked like a man.

All were farmers. They worked the land and reaped the yields. The dry womb of the earth turned green with their wheat and fennel, mustard, cumin, and fenugreek. After Independence, these mighty farmers had done well. They cast seeds in the dirt with their eyes closed and then gathered up the fruits. The five looked as if they had been born not of woman's flesh but from the earth's own womb. As if they had grown up and blossomed among the kareel, aak, khejari, and acacia trees. As if the grass, the trees, the shrubs, the flowers were their kin.

The five were brothers, cousins of near about the same stock. They were going to Jodhpur to buy a tractor. Each had bundles of rupee notes stashed in the undershirt pocket at his breast. The heat of it made their faces glow. The roots of wealth may lie deep in the heart, but the sheen of such invisible fruits shines clear for all to see.

They stepped off the bus with their hands in their pockets and headed off, their strides long and brisk, towards the tractor showroom as arranged. If it were in their power, they wouldn't have let their feet even touch that pavement black as rot. Once they reached the showroom, they recognized the owner through the window. As soon as their eyes fell on his shiny bald pate they cried, 'We're in luck! Omji himself is here today.'

A blast of ice-cold air rushed over them as soon as they pulled open the door. They walked into the shop, and one sighed, 'Here he's enjoying heaven, while we toil like beasts of burden.'

Omji smiled a thin smile and said in a delighted voice, 'If you want to exchange your farm for my shop, I wouldn't object.'

'Hah! You'd regret it!'

'That remains to be seen.'

The eldest cousin scolded them, 'We've only just walked in the door and already you're talking about regrets. Each person must follow his own fate, and do the work that suits him best.'

Sitting on those cushiony chairs felt like sitting on nothing. They poked and prodded the soft cushions two, three times to make sure the seats would hold their weight.

Satisfied, they settled into the chairs, elbows on the armrests. After the perfunctory duas and salaams, one of the cousins began, 'Somehow or the other our number has finally come. We need to have the tractor today. We started out this morning at an auspicious hour. We need to return to our village before the day is done. We would consider it a favour if you could arrange for it somehow.'

'Every customer I meet makes the same demand. You have waited more than two years, and now you cannot even wait two more days?'

The youngest cousin said, 'Two days would be too long. At this point we cannot wait another two hours. Our women have been standing at the doors ever since we left this morning, watching for our return to bless the tractor. Charge a little extra if you have to, but you must deliver it today!'

Omji smiled at their impatience, then said, 'I know how you rustics are. I made sure the tractor was ready yesterday. Take it whenever you wish.'

Their joy knew no bounds. It was as if they had suddenly been handed the whole world to rule! The middle cousin looked at Omji's head shining like the moon and said, 'How could a man with such a lucky brow ever shirk his work? May you live long.'

The cousins were familiar with Omji. One or the other would visit him from time to time to check their number on the waiting list. He became as friendly with them as the business demanded. His manner was easy, his words pleasant. Every bit of him looked like it had been manufactured in a factory, like the parts of the tractor. There was a bald spot where a bald spot should be, fringed on three sides with thinning hair. A neck where a neck should be. A smile as the occasion required.

He scanned the five faces before him and said, 'You must be relieved. You've spent your whole day bouncing up and down inside a bus. Now sit back and relax, have some cold water,' and he reached for his buzzer as he continued to make polite conversation. A man came in at once. Omji asked him to bring some lassis. When the man disappeared, he began apologizing, 'I will not be able to offer anything to rival what you have in your village. The milk here is water-thin. The curds will turn your stomach. All you get in cities is cooled air, icy water, soft cushions, and bright lights. The grandiosity of the adulterated and the ostentation of the fake. You cannot find good grain and spices at any price. I am ashamed to offer you anything at all.'

One of the cousins laughed and said, 'If you really mean to offer, there are plenty of luxuries to be had around here. The envy of the gods above. Otherwise, we'll just have to cool down with a lassi instead.'

The hint was clear enough. Omji laughed loudly and said, 'No, we cannot have any of that here in the store. But if you can wait till evening, I will be able to offer you real hospitality at my home.'

'Your invitation alone is enough, Omji! Where's our tractor? Let's just take a quick peek.'

'First, have your lassis and then we'll go down and have a look.'

'The lassis aren't going to run away, are they? The sight of the tractor will cool us down. Then the lassis will taste sweeter.'

Omji went with them himself. The tractor stood ready in the workshop. A blood-red Massey Ferguson, vivid as a mound of birbahuti bugs. The sight of it made them flush in their hearts. They patted the tractor and inspected it closely. Then they all went back to the office. Their glasses of lassi were sitting on the table, carefully covered.

Omji eased himself back into his chair and began musing, 'How times have changed! There used to be just one thakur who ruled over the area. But now you big peasants have become the new thakurs. You are the ones who have really taken advantage of Independence. Where before people used to dream of having buttermilk, now they order all the luxuries as if they were water. In the old days people couldn't even afford a plough and a spade, but now no one even gives a second thought to spending thousands of rupees on a tractor. Yaar, enjoy this independence, have as much fun as you can, don't even think twice.'

The fourth cousin interrupted him. 'I wouldn't call this khak fun! Nothing to eat but grain, and you barely fill your belly. We've suffered for a thousand generations. Now the one-eyed lady puts on make-up and you begrudge her airs? Thanks to Gandhi baba we actually live like human beings now. How else would our villages have got all those motors, tractors, and radios?'

'And soon we'll have to fill our stomachs with paper notes. Before too long we won't even be able to buy grain.'

'You just keep giving us tractors, and we'll keep giving you grain. Draw up a contract if you like.'

The eldest cousin spoke up. 'No one gives anything to anyone just like that. The water buffalo grazes only to fill its own belly. Everyone everywhere wracks his brain just to find a way to meet his own needs. One does it by selling a tractor, and another by buying it.' When his words reached his own ears the eldest cousin realized his talk had gone down the wrong path and he tried to steer the conversation back to better terrain by adding, 'Still, what you say is true. Due to Gandhi baba's grace, we're better off since Independence. Heaps of grain in every home, milk and curds flowing freely....'

Omji began shaking his bald head and cut in, 'No, not in every home, that's not true. It's only a small number of you big farmers who have all you could want.'

The youngest cousin had been to college. He said, 'What do you mean *all* we could want? The best you can say is that the jaws of misery's grip have loosened a little. Just enough to give us room to breathe. But happiness is still as distant as the moon.'

Wanting to put an end to all this nonsense, the middle cousin said, 'What's the use of wishing for the moon? Let's get down to business. Take the money out of your pockets to give it to Omji so we can get our goods and return. We're wasting time talking.'

Suddenly they remembered why they had come. A moment later their hands were in their pockets, pulling out rupee notes, piling them on the table. A fifty horsepower foreign-built tractor with trolley, harrow, and plough. A sixty-thousand-rupee transaction.

Omji got busy counting the money and putting it away in his drawer while the five cousins all stood up at the same time and went down to the garage for their merchandise.

The eldest cousin sent the youngest off to the bazaar for garlands, mounds of gur, rum, and bright red gulal powder. The four cousins helped to load the plough and harrow on to the trailer. They had just caught their breath when the youngest returned. They celebrated by passing around the gur and festooning the tractor's hood with marigold garlands. Then they painted a gleaming red swastika on the front of the hood in gulal. The youngest three were able drivers.

The day had passed quickly. The sun was just about to slip behind its western veil. From the Ajmer–Jodhpur toll gate the road looked clear, smooth, and wide. The garlands fluttered in the breeze to the rhythm of the engine's roar. Sitting atop the tractor the five cousins felt as if heaven itself were gliding beneath their wheels. And the earth curving towards the horizon before them seemed punier than a coconut shell. As if the sinking sun had paused in the sky just to gaze at them. As if the thrumming wind were trying to sweep away any inauspiciousness. All the happiness in the world tossed inside their hearts. Even the long journey of the setting sun's rays seemed to be made worthwhile at the touch of the goddess sparkling in their pendants. The tractor's clanging sent birds hidden in roadside thickets and trees flying in all directions. But to the cousins, it was their own happiness taking wing.

Suddenly a shrill cry broke into their reverie. They looked around, startled. A hawk was swooping down, wings spread wide, on a baby hare it had spotted hiding in the brush. It seized the trembling body in its talons and soared upwards, back into the sky. The cousins smiled and looked at one another. The eldest observed, 'One's fate can never be postponed. It was destined that his death should take place in this very bush, by this very hawk, at this very moment.' They gazed into the sky until the hawk faded away. The tractor continued to roar along the road. They were approaching a small overpass. The fourth cousin urged the driver on, 'As much as we're hurrying, we're still running late. So far everything has been auspicious—there were good omens when we left the village.'

A steep slope lay just ahead. As they came over the crest they noticed a cyclist riding on the road, a few furlongs ahead. The cyclist heard the roar of the engine and turned to look behind him. A tractor coming. He turned back and began pedalling furiously. The men sitting in the tractor noticed him speed up and watched as the gap between them widened. The youngest cousin was at the wheel. He muttered, 'Fool! Pedal as fast as you like, you'll never beat a tractor!' He gave the throttle a little tug, and it roared even louder.

The engine's roar rattled louder in the cyclist's ears. He pedalled faster, and the gap widened again. The driver couldn't stand to see the distance between them. He accelerated even more, saying, 'Little mother-lover! He'll tire out in the end, let him enjoy his little triumph while he can.' The middle cousin added, 'You never know what's going on inside the skulls of those bareheaded punks.'

The tractor was racing along by now. The garlands began flapping even more wildly. The eldest cousin agreed, 'Of course he'll wear out. Why bother speeding up? A poor cycle can't compete with a tractor!'

A piercing shriek struck their ears as a hawk swooped down from the sky and pounced on a mouse scurrying desperately to get to his hole underground. A moment later, the shrieks faded away. The sun was half-sunken. Now the sun would also disappear for the night. Scarlet light radiated from the setting sun, red as gulal, as if reflecting the tractor's red gleam. The brothers turned from the setting sun and looked at the road ahead. Arrey! He was even further ahead! The same thought pinched everyone inside: a two-hundred-rupee cycle against a sixty-thousand-rupee tractor. No match! Does a mouse dare to wrestle an elephant?

The second cousin spat out, 'If he pumps those pedals till his lungs burst, it's his family he'll be leaving behind.' The fourth cousin said, 'Ram only knows when he'll leave his family behind; all I can see is that he's leaving our tractor in the dirt.' The youngest cousin eased out the throttle a little more. The tractor was brand new. It wasn't good to race along at full throttle.

The cyclist looked back. He had quite a lead now. And his exhilaration made him pedal even faster. His feet were spinning round and round like reels. The cycle slipped down the road as easy as water down a mountainside. As if the cyclist had turned into a whirlwind, or even that he were riding a whirlwind.

All the eyes on the tractor were riveted on the cyclist. Quite a gap lay between them now. And it was only growing wider. A foreign tractor. Worth sixty thousand rupees. Festooned with marigold malas. And a two-paisa cycle! A college punk. Head bare. Wearing shorts.

A sharp gust of wind snapped one of the garland threads. The garland began to flap around. Doubling up, unfurling straight. Another garland snapped. The tractor driver felt every thump of the marigold garland on the hood like a thorny cane beating against his breast. He ground his teeth together and pulled the throttle out to the limit. The tractor catapulted forward like a shot from a cannon. The sound of the revving engine echoed in the air. The sky that moments ago seemed to be falling beneath their wheels now seemed to be rising higher and higher over them.

The gap began to close. Even more. Ah, now they were really close.

The world seemed as small as a coconut, reduced to two little dots. The tractor. The bicycle. A sixty-thousand-rupee machine. And a two-paisa piece of junk.

As it happened, two army trucks came bumping down the road from the other direction just at that moment and the tractor was forced to slow down. The cyclist saw his chance and clipped ahead.

The middle cousin said, 'These city punks are worthless! Taking advantage of a chance like that!' The eldest cousin said, 'If the poor fellow wants to show off for now, then let him. How long can he carry on like this? He's bound to run out of breath. Pagla, squandering his energies like this. Once his internal piping starts sagging, he won't even be able to do it with his woman. Were such drives meant to be spent on a cycle?'

Now that the road was clear the youngest cousin opened up the throttle. Like gunpowder suddenly touched with a spark. The tractor was like a dust storm trying to catch the wind. And gradually the gap began to diminish.

The cyclist heard the tractor just behind him and looked around. He snapped his head forward in a fury. And his feet began to spin like reels. They became speed itself, speed and nothing else.

Now he had begun to sweat. He was the fastest cyclist in all of Rajasthan. And, yes, he was also a man. Arms where arms should be, legs where legs should be. Breath where breath should be. Dreams where dreams should be. He had been working out on his bicycle, sixty or seventy miles a day for the past two months. If he came first in the All India Bicycle Championship next month, then he might get to go to Paris. He felt confident enough after two months of dedicated training. But today's little contest would prove it for certain. He clenched his teeth and poured all his strength into spinning the pedals.

He went to college with a young woman who had fallen in love with him the first time she saw him race and proposed to him. But he had not been able to reply with a forthright 'yes' or 'no'. They kept meeting and talking and spending time together, and once they had begun to know each other in their souls, it became clear what they had to do. He had promised to marry her as soon as the All India Championship was over. He had been raised in tight circumstances. And she had grown up in a house of plenty. But they lived only for one another. They ate as if with the same mouth. And on their priceless wedding night the moon would smile on their bridal bed.

Suddenly her face appeared before his eyes. As if she had turned into the breeze to watch the race. His vigour increased tenfold. As if his feet had grown wings. What power did that lifeless tractor have compared to the shimmery image of his beloved? The cyclist pulled further and further ahead. Before long, the distance between them had doubled.

Now the tractor was at full throttle. They could do no more. Their insides started writhing. The whistling wind was being swallowed up by the roar of the engine. Their reign over the whole world had been grabbed from their hands in a dash. The new tractor shot down the road like a cannonball. It looked as if a whirlwind had taken over that bareheaded boy's feet. His beloved's face shone before his eyes. The distance grew and grew. His lungs didn't quaver, and his breath didn't break.

Half of the marigold garlands had snapped and fallen. But what could the cousins do?

No one can see what the ephemeral future holds. Suddenly the feet fast as a whirlwind were spinning emptily. The chain had come off. Still the boy didn't worry. He figured his feet could match the tractor's speed. Images of his beloved's face surrounded him. There could be no greater power than this in the world. He stopped the cycle and quickly dismounted. He leaned the bicycle on the kickstand and patiently began putting the chain back on.

Slowly the distance was decreasing. The air could not contain the tractor's roar, nor the five cousins' happiness. Well, who knows when luck will smile on you? It didn't matter how, but this sixty-thousand-rupee matter of honour was saved. If people want to deceive themselves into believing in fraudulent victories, then who would stop them?

The tractor's roar sounded closer. It was taking much too long to get the chain back on in the flurry. Before long the tractor was right there. And still he had confidence in his strength and the power of his beloved's face before him.

The tractor roared past. All five cousins shouted out words typically human as they sped by. A flock of crows began cawing overhead as if in one voice. The voices of the humans couldn't be heard over the cawing of the crows and the roar of the engine.

The tractor was already one or two farm-lengths ahead when the cyclist got the chain back in place and started off again. Four of the cousins turned back to watch him. They thought to themselves, the bastard was just pretending his chain came off! Maybe the race was too much for him.

But the chain was back on, and he had turned into a tornado again. The distance between them slowly began to decrease as he came closer and closer.

The scenery was beginning to merge with the darkness. The four cousins were straining to see the boy behind them. He was gaining ground!

Now it was an all-out race. The tractor couldn't go any faster. They gnashed their teeth. The red of the tractor began to dissolve in the fading light. The youngest cousin asked, 'Where is that harami now?'

The fourth cousin said through clenched teeth, 'Looks like he's going to pull ahead.'

'Hah! Even his father wouldn't have dreamed of it!' As he said this, the youngest cousin started to hear first the hawk's shrieks, then the mouse's squeals, echoing in his ears in turns. After a moment the shrieks were in one ear, the squeals in the other, and wouldn't stop. It seemed as if the entire universe were about to rip apart. The tractor's roar got swallowed up in that echo.

A whole different world was glittering in the eyes of the cyclist. Everywhere he looked, images of his beloved's face were twinkling—in the soft scattering of stars, in the trees and shrubs, in the sand dunes, in the tractor's trolley up ahead. Today would be the test. If he could get ahead of the tractor, then he would get married as soon as possible. Tomorrow, if she agreed. If not, then the day after. Or the day after that. Whenever she wanted. Why wait to pass them? All the world was in the palm of his hand. The warp and woof of golden dreams was being woven in front of his eyes.

Meanwhile, the hawk's shrieks and the mouse's squeals were smothering every particle of air. The four cousins shouted through clenched teeth, 'That bare-headed fellow is making us lick the dirt off our turbans!'

Then they came up with a new plan. 'Make the tractor swerve as soon as he gets close. What will the little harami have to say to that....' The hawk's shrieks and the mouse's squeals had now found human voices.

And meanwhile the images of his beloved's face began growing brighter and brighter. Each image became more and more distinct.

Now he had moved up, beside the trolley. The shrieks and squeals hid themselves away in the driver's head and assumed a posture of silence.

The next moment the speeding cyclist crashed into the tractor. Lightning flashed before his eyes and the lights of his beloved's faces extinguished one by one. The tractor's rear tyre passed over his bare head, mashing it into chutney. The rest of the faces were snuffed out.

A human voice hissed once more in the wind, 'Mother-lover, he had nerve trying to overtake a tractor!'

The youngest cousin had been to college. He pulled the tractor over, grabbed a bottle out of a sack and said, 'Let's give the poor guy some rum!'

Then he went over to him, walking on two legs like a man. Opened the bottle above the cyclist. Emptied half the bottle of rum into the boy's mouth. Then he broke the bottle near the boy's head and ran back to the tractor. The tractor roared as he took off. The women must be standing in the doorway waiting for them. How happy they would be to see them return!

Human laughter echoed in the wind.

A picture was left behind them on the road, waiting for expert appraisal. Brain-white smudges on a blood-red background. Shards of broken glass. A man's dead body. White shorts. Bloodied sky-blue undershirt. Mashed dreams. Streams of love. The painting wasn't bad!

But...paintings of the two World Wars, pictures of Hiroshima and Nagasaki, of Vietnam, of Bangladesh...those are the true masterpieces. Compared to this one, those are so much more refined, so much more complex and nuanced. This one doesn't compare. Still, considering it was done by a band of rustics, it wasn't so bad.

Yes, the five were only men. Each man spoke like a man. Each man walked like a man.

SEED

Mahasweta Devi

TRANSLATED FROM THE BENGALI BY IPSITA CHANDA

The land north of Kuruda and Hesadi villages is uneven, and so arid and sun-baked that there is not a hint of grass even after the rains. You might see the occasional erect serpent hoods of cactus plants, and a few neem trees. In the middle of this scorched wasteland, where no cattle graze, is a low-lying boat-shaped piece of land. Around half a bigha. You can spot this bit of land only if you climb a high embankment; the splash of green, from the wild aloe bushes that grow on the land, presents an eerie sight.

Even more sinister is the machan in the middle of the field, a platform on wooden posts topped by a thatched hut. A hut on the land is most unsettling for anyone who sees it, because such a hut is generally built to guard crops. Only stray aloe plants grow here, with leaves as thorny as the plant of the pineapple. Even buffaloes don't eat them. Elsewhere in the world, the fibre from these plants makes extremely strong ropes. In India, they are dismissed as wild bushes.

The most eerie scene occurs as evening falls. A man comes striding along from Kuruda village. As he approaches, you can see that he's old, his skin gnarled and knotted, a loincloth wrapped around his waist, a quilted bag hanging from it. He carries a stick and raps the aloe barks at random as he approaches the machan. He climbs the rickety ladder fastened to the branches of the tree. He strikes a flint stone, lights a bidi, and sits down on the machan. Every day. When night falls, he spreads a mat and goes to sleep. Every night.

At this time, every day, in Kuruda village, the old wife of Dulan Ganju yells curses at him. This is her right. Because this old man is Dulan Ganju. Her son, daughter-in-law, and grandchildren dislike this yelling and cursing, but can't do anything about it. If they protest, they'll be abused too. And in these parts, Dhatua's mother's abusive powers are legendary. In every dispute, she is called upon to exhibit her professional squabbling skills. She takes the field and starts by cursing the first of the adversary's seven previous generations. Generally, by the time she reaches the third generation, the opposition flees the field.

She is widely respected. When there was trouble at Tamadih during the Emergency, the police had come to this village asking questions. Dhatua's mother's fiery tongue had forced them to leave. One of the fugitives the police was seeking was hiding in the loft of the cowshed. Dhatua's mother's strident commands to 'Come, search every room, you vultures!' conclusively proved that the whole village was completely innocent.

She didn't stop there. 'Look,' she said, 'there are only children and the elderly in the village. Want to examine them? Want to arrest them?'

Once the police left, Dhatua's mother bloodied the fugitive with her sharp tongue, 'Rotoni! You've always been a halfwit! Less sense than a nanny goat! So you axed a Rajput mahajan? Excellent, well done. You should've despatched the devil by giving it to him in the neck. Why didn't you hide in the jungle? Which idiot returns to his village? Go, go to the forest!'

Dhatua and Latua don't have the guts to tell their mother, 'Don't curse our Baba.'

If they do, Ma will explode. So, the old man is now his sons' darling, and their mother a worthless old she-goat! Do the sons know their father's true character? Only she knows.

Ma had been married at the age of four. At fourteen, after the gaona ceremony when she attained puberty, she made her husband's family her home. Ma knew the old man through and through. Lord of a thorny wasteland, guarding his land alone. After all, who would be widowed if a snake bit him or a tiger dragged him off? Dhatua and Latua? Could they fool the government into giving them seeds every year for that barren piece of land? Collect government fertilizer and sell it off? Extract money from the government for the maintenance of a plough and buffalo borrowed from the pahaan, the village priest, year after year?

The sons fall silent. Ma puffs away at her hookah, and delivering her final, unanswerable line, 'You'll never know my true worth till I'm dead,' goes off to sleep. The daughters-in-law whisper to the sons, 'Well, another day gone.'

Ma addresses the darkness, 'One day he'll lie there dead. I won't even be here.'

The sons know it is abnormal to guard the aloe plants every night. But they don't consider their father a normal person by any standards. Baba is a dark character, complicated and impossible to understand. The trade of the Ganju caste is skinning dead animals. Baba poisoned a few buffaloes that belonged to the powerful Rajput mahajan, Lachman Singh, owner of ten rifles. This in Lachman Singh's own village, Tamadih. Then he sold the skins. Characteristically, Lachman suspected his traditional rival, his brother and co-heir Daitari Singh of the crime. The resultant family feud is still raging.

Despite this, Baba survives, proving that he is a man of a different measure. Always busy with such strategies of survival, he had never had time for his sons or grandsons.

Ma is no less. Her mature old bones have such stamina, bear such stubborn courage and resentment, that she, too, is beyond the ordinary measure of a human being.

Their sons had never seen their father and mother seated together chatting. But when Baba is planning something important, he asks Ma to come and sit in the courtyard. Lights her hookah and says, 'Eh Dhatua ke ma! Advise me. Give me your advice. Everyone in the village consults you, even the police are scared of you.'

'What mischief are you brewing now? Who're you planning to cheat or rob?'

Ma's voice is loud, but without rancour. Together they plot and plan in low voices. Such an event occurs once a year or every year and a half.

At other times, Baba doesn't pay any attention to Ma. She says, 'I might as well go back to my father's house.'

Baba smiles slyly and quietly tells the breeze, 'Yes. To that huge mansion of your father's in Tura village.'

Ma has no father-mother-brothers. Yet she gives Baba the opportunity to smile crookedly and pass mocking remarks.

This is what Latua and Dhatua's parents are like—and there's nothing to be done about it. Just as you can't help the fact that the hill lies to the west, or that the Kuruda River flows nearby. Sanichari says, 'Your father and mother are both mad. Your father, of course, is completely crazy. Why else would he guard that land without ever farming it? Why?'

There's a proverb which says that what you pick up free is worth fourteen annas. The land was free, but there wasn't even fourteen paise profit from it.

The land belongs to Lachman Singh. Quite a few years ago, activists belonging to the Sarvodaya Movement, which sought to redistribute land from the rich to the poor, had gone from door to door to every landlord in this area. About them too, Sanichari used to say, 'These are madmen of the babu caste. They'll make the landlords feel deep regret and spontaneously admit, "Tch, tch! We have so much land, and they have none at all?" And they'll give away the land. The day they do this, I'll sit on a divan, eat butter and cream, and cook rice twice a day.'

But some landlords did begin to give away little bits of stony, barren land to provoke their fellow landlords into doing the same. Everyone had 500 or 700 or 1,000 or 2,000 bighas of fertile land. Everyone harvested paddy or maize or maroa or mustard or arhar. Groundnuts earned large profits. So it didn't really matter much if you gave away some land.

The Sarvodaya leaders and workers had become the butt of their countrymen's mockery. The gifts of land saved their face. Didn't the upper caste Rajput and Kayastha mahajans, jotedars who owned or controlled the land in the Kuruda belt, give up their lands? Didn't that mean they had had a change of heart? Certainly. Bas. The Sarvodaya mission was successful. Immediately after this, the activists would go off to change the hearts of the dacoits in Madhya Pradesh. Their mission would not be complete till they filled the hearts of two classes—the landlords and the dacoits—with remorse.

The gifting of land has many uses. It is a way of getting rid of barren land and buying over its recipients. It strengthens one's position with the government. Above all, like a rasgulla after a meal, there is the added satisfaction of knowing one is compassionate.

Dulan Ganju gets this land. He didn't want to take it. But Lachman Singh is too powerful. His eyes grew red with anger and he said, 'Typical of you low castes! Today I'm feeling generous, so I'm giving you this. Fool, do you think I'll feel this way tomorrow?'

Dulan said, 'Hujoor is my mai-baap.'

'Then? Low-lying land floods every monsoon, sow whatever you like and you'll get high yields.'

During the monsoons, reddish water streams down the embankment and collects in the field. But all around lay barren, stony ground. Who'll go all that way to plough that land? If it was fertile land, would Lachman Singh have let it lie fallow? Dulan had gone to borrow money. He came back a landlord.

Everyone in the village said, 'It's a rich man's whim! He eats parathas soaked in ghee, and the heat's gone to his head. He'll forget all about it tomorrow.'

'Suppose he doesn't?'

'Just let the land be. In Ara-Chhapra, this is the kind of land they gave at the behest of the Sarvodayis. Those who got it sold it back to the mahajan or mortgaged it to him. You'll do the same.'

'Who'll take that land? The mahajan's buying himself a

good name, and at the same time getting rid of it.'

Dulan would have said more, but the pahaan who was part of his audience gave him a mighty tongue-lashing. People had so many problems to deal with, what was Dulan's land trouble in comparison?

Dulan mutters and grumbles.

His wife says, 'Oh! He's busy calculating how to make a profit from this land, but just look at the fuss he's making! No one's ever seen through his wiles.'

'Profit from the land?'

The next day, Sanichari hears all about it and says, 'Why? Eh, Dhatua ke maiya! If he gets land, Dhatua ke baap can go to Tohri! To the block development office! The government will bear the expenses of farming, seeds, everything!'

Only when he heard this did Dulan smile. His eyes glazed over with dreams. Even a man like Dulan had not realized how barren land could help him run his household. In some fairy tales, cows yield milk even though they haven't calved.

⸎

One day, the land came into Dulan's possession in the form of documents and deeds. They had two adjacent rooms and a corridor in the Ganju neighbourhood: rooms that served as a living room, kitchen, everything. This was his world. Barricaded, one end of the corridor turned into a bedroom for husband and wife. Someone so bereft of support generally has no backbone. All around him were Rajput jotedars and mahajans; the Brahman priest Hanuman Misra of Tahar was particularly influential in these parts. Living in such an area, continuously under the thumb of the higher castes, would naturally break the spirit of people like Dulan who belonged to the lower Ganju and Dushad castes.

But the drive for survival prompted him to exploit situations by using his natural guile rather than force. He fooled his powerful adversaries not by strength, but by wit and cunning. All the stratagems of survival were at his fingertips.

Dhatua's mother says, 'It's a large piece of land, very fertile. Oh, Dhatua, tell your baba to build a granary for his crops. Oh, Latua-re, your father's become a zamindar, yes, a zamindar!'

She said all this, but the villagers and she continued to wait to see what Dulan would do.

The villagers were appreciative witnesses to Dulan's one-man strategic warfare. Everyone knew about the business of Lachman Singh's buffaloes, but no one told on Dulan. He sold a pumpkin to Daitari Singh's household and took money from both Daitari's wife and mother. When the bananas and radishes were brought in a bullock cart from Lachman Singh's house to the banks of the Kuruda River during the Chhat festival, he walked beside the cart, shooing away imaginary birds, and continuously stealing things. Not once had he ever given a single thing to the other villagers. Yet, they treated him with respect. He could do what they dared not do.

As soon as he got the land, Dulan touched Lachman Singh's knees and said, 'Malik, protector! You've given me land, but how will I farm it? I won't get a thing from the BD office. A-ha-ha, such a good piece of land! I've got it, but I can't use it.'

'Why? The BD office will give you everything.'

'No, Hujoor, I'm a low caste.'

'Of course you are. It's because you don't remember this that you get kicked around. Sure, you're a low caste! But how can they refuse to help someone *I'm* giving land to? Who's the BD babu?'

'Kayastha, Hujoor. Says the Rajputs are stupid country bumpkins. Listens to the radio all the time and uses his left hand to drink water, tea.'

'Arrey Ram! Chee, chee, chee.'

'I've seen it myself, Hujoor.'

'I'll write to him.'

Lachman Singh is no learned mahapundit. He keeps a vakil. The vakil writes a strong appeal in Kayathi* Hindi advocating that Dulan get money in instalments to buy a plough and bullock, seeds and fertilizer. The BDO might live in Tohri, and it's true that Tohri is far from Lachman's village Tamadih, but he has only one life. The SDO himself has warned him to avoid conflicts with Lachman and Hanuman Misra. So he immediately agreed to everything. He explained to the loincloth-clad Dulan in a very gentle voice that he would get seeds and fertilizer. But he wouldn't get the entire amount for the plough and bullock at one go. If he could pay an advance and show that he had bought the plough and bullock, he would get the rest of the money.

Dulan returned to the village and said to the pahaan, 'The sarkar makes laws, but doesn't understand anything. People buy ploughs and bullocks with cash. Who will sell to someone who pays in instalments? Lend me your plough and bullock.'

---

*Local variant of Hindi, used for legal documents.

Dulan got the money by displaying that plough and bullock every alternate year. Every time he asks the BDO for the money, he says, 'The bullock died, Hujoor.'

He takes the money. Collects the fertilizer and sells it at Tohri itself. Hoists the sack of seeds onto his shoulder and brings it home.

He eats the seeds.

It's no easy task to boil paddy seeds and make rice. But he does it. The first time, his wife had said, 'So much seed! How much land do you have?'

'You can't measure it even if you try.'

'What do you mean?'

'Our hunger. Can hunger be measured? The land of the stomach keeps expanding! You want me to farm that barren strip of land? Are you crazy?'

'What'll you do, then?'

'Boil it, grind it, we'll eat it.'

'Are you going to kill yourself eating seeds?'

'We haven't died yet. Didn't we eat rats during the famine? Why should we die from eating seeds? If we do, at least we'll have died eating rice! We'll go to heaven.'

It took Dhatua's mother just one meal of rice made from the seeds to realize that she had never eaten anything so sweet in her life.

She proudly told everyone in the village about this tasty food. Can any other married woman in the village boast of how brainy her man is, of how cunningly he fooled the gorment so that his family could eat paddy-rice seeds?

Everyone in the village was pleased. The gorment has never protected their interests. The gorment's BDO never helps them with farming. Their children never get to enter the gorment's primary school. Lachman Singh or Daitari Singh force them to harvest their crops for four annas a day or a single meal, at gunpoint. There was a lot of tension over this, because the Ganju-Dushad-Dhobis of the neighbouring block were getting kicked and fed for eight annas daily. The villagers wanted a raise of twenty-five paise. Knowing all this, whenever there was trouble, the SDO brought in police reinforcements and picked up the labourers. Lachman Singh and Daitari were let off without a word.

The gorment belongs to Lachman Singh. The gorment belongs to Lachman Singh, Daitari Singh, Hanuman Misra. If such a gorment is fleeced by someone who happens to be a Dulan Ganju, then the villagers are bound to appreciate it.

Like the mythical Kamadhenu, the cow that never ceased giving, the land continues to yield Dulan about six hundred rupees annually. But Dulan continued to sleep outdoors. At the corner of the covered veranda, on a platform beside Dhatua's mother, who coughs and wheezes as if she has asthma. They tie a billy goat beneath the platform when they go to sleep. A son to a room, each with his wife and children. Wheat, maroa, corncobs by the sacksful, pots and pans, firewood, everything stacked in the same room. The earnings from the land cannot see them through the whole year, so father and sons work as field labourers, or search the forest for wild potatoes, or carry headloads in Tohri, or work in Misraji's orchards. Like everyone else.

One day, Karan Dusadh of Tamadih arrived in the village. A glamorous personality who used to work as a labourer in Lachman's field. He had a dispute over wages with the owner-manager, the malik, and went to jail at Hazaribagh where he made friends with prisoners from other parts of Bihar. They didn't shrink from him because he was a low-caste Dusadh. They respected him as a fighter. They were amazed that with no organizational help at all, two hundred labourers had turned against an ocean of exploitation and set fire to the powerful Lachman Singh's fields of ripened wheat. They explained to him the importance of battles like theirs, burgeoning everywhere. The need to fight in an organized way. The need to fight from their own base.

The repercussions were swift and merciless. They were tortured. They were beaten up by the authorities. Many were even beaten to death. Despite all this, they told Karan, 'You're a fighter, you did the right thing, never give up the fight.'

Hence, there was turmoil in the layers of Karan Dusadh's mind. The Karan who had rebelled only when Lachman Singh had driven him to the end of his tether, now came out of jail and said to everyone, 'Conditions are unchanged. Why wait till he forces us to resist, get shot at, get jailed? Let's organize in advance. Talk things over with him. Ask the police to be present during harvesting. Our demands are very few. We're Harijans and Adivasis. We won't get good wages in these parts. We'll fight for eight annas. Women-men-children, eight annas for everyone. He's giving four annas. This will be our "twenty-five-paise battle" for an additional four annas.'

As soon as Dulan heard about this, he called Karan to Kuruda. Suspicious by nature, he insisted they talk on the embankment at the edge of his land, away from everyone. Karan Dusadh is middle-aged, scrawny, a tiny man. After two years with the prisoners in Hazaribagh, he is like a new person.

'All this caste business is rubbish. It's the Brahman and the wealthy who have spun these tales about untouchability.'

His words startle Dulan. For a moment he is speechless. Then—he's an old fox, after all!—'Oh, the babus who can read and write have always said that. Now let's get down to business. That Lachman Singh and the BDO, SDO and daroga, the police chief, drink together. First, go to the Adivasi office and the Harijan Seva Sangh at Tohri. Keep them informed. Let them go with you to the thana and the SDO.'

'Why? Are we that weak?'

'Yes, we are, Karan. Make no mistake. The entire sarkar will help Lachman. He can open fire and they won't notice. But you raise a stick and they'll catch you. Madanlalji of the Harijan Seva Sangh is a good man. Everyone knows him. Get him to back you.'

Karan takes this advice. Madanlal can garner a powerful pool of votes. So the SDO and daroga secretly consult with Lachman Singh. Then they agree to what Madanlal says.

The harvesting and gathering of the corn goes on without incident. Eight annas as wages. Karan Dusadh becomes a hero. A fairy tale come true.

Then, abruptly, Lachman tells Dulan, 'Stay on your land tomorrow. If anyone gets to know that I've told you this, I'll kill you.'

When this 'tomorrow' turns into 'today' at daybreak, the SDO suddenly goes off to Ranchi and the daroga to far-off Purudiha, chasing bandits.

As evening turns to dusk, in the radiance of the setting sun, Lachman Singh, accompanied by his Rajput-caste brothers, attacks the Dusadh quarters in Tamadih.

Fires rage, people burn, huts collapse.

At night, the newly risen moon reveals an unearthly silent scene before Dulan's eyes. Lachman Singh on horseback. Two horses tied abreast, a plank across their backs, laden with two corpses. Ten of Lachman's men escort the landlord.

At the point of Lachman's gun, Dulan buries Karan and his peaceable brother Bulaki in his land. Terrified, head bowed, he digs deep holes with his shovel. Lachman stands on the edge of the field, supervising and chewing paan. Then he says, 'Breathe a word of this to anyone, you cur, and you'll join Karan Dusadh. We can't trust the jackals and wolves not to dig up the corpses. Build a machan here tomorrow. Stay on guard at night. I'm the son of a Rajput! Karan lit this fire—from now on, there'll be more dead bodies.'

Dulan nods. In order to survive, he says, 'As you wish.'

The police came the next day to investigate the attack. A lot of hullabaloo. Ultimately it was learnt that Karan wasn't even present during the disturbance; the reporters' attempts to write 'A True Harijan Story' at all costs were totally foiled. No one said a word against Lachman Singh. One of his henchmen spent a few days in jail for arson. The government gave a pittance in compensation to those rendered homeless for the construction of new huts.

From then on, Dulan sleeps on the land. At first, this is seen as a sign of insanity, and his sons try to dissuade him. No advice penetrates Dulan's ears at this stage. When questioned, he glowers silently at them with bloodshot eyes. Then, shaking his head, he threatens them with his stick, 'Don't talk to me, Dhatua! I'll break your head.'

A great explosion, a landslide, occurs in the strata of his mind, ending in mental upheaval. So easy! Is everything so easy for the Lachmans? Dulan had thought that just as a man's life is linked to so many rites and rituals, so is his death. But Lachman Singh has proved that these time-honoured customs are meaningless. How easy! Two corpses on horseback! And these corpses must have been carried off arrogantly, from right under the Tamadih Dusadhs' noses. Lachman knows there's no need to hide them. Witnesses won't say a thing. They have read the warning in Lachman's sharp, silent gaze. He who opens his mouth will die. This has happened before. And will happen again. Once in a while it is necessary to rend the sky with leaping flames and the screams of the dying, just to remind the Harijans and untouchables that government laws, appointment of officers, and constitutional decrees are nothing. Rajputs remain Rajputs, Brahmans remain Brahmans and Dusadh-Chamar-Ganju-Dhobi remain lower than Brahman-Kayastha-Rajput-Bhumihar-Kurmi. The Rajput or Brahman or Kayastha or Bhumihar or Yadav or Kurmi is, in places, as poor as, or even poorer than, the Harijan. But they are not tossed into the flames because of their caste. The fire god, having tasted the flesh of forest-dwelling, black-skinned outcastes during the burning of the Khandava forest*, is fond of the taste of the untouchable poor.

All this causes havoc in Dulan's mind. Before this, his was a surface cunning. Aimed at survival. Now he has to conceal two corpses beneath his heart. They begin to rot within him. Buried in the earth, Karan and Bulaki grow

---

*A forest mentioned in the Mahabharata.

lighter as they gradually lose the burden of flesh. But in the realm of Dulan's mind, the corpses weigh heavy. He looks wan, hardly speaks. He can't confide in anyone. The constant burden he bears makes him feel as if he is tied to a whipping post. If he opens his mouth, the Dusadh quarters of Kuruda will go up in flames, ashes will scatter in the air, along with the stench of charred flesh.

Slowly time passes. Everyone is forced to forget that two people, Karan and Bulaki, went missing. From Tohri to Burudiha on one side and Phuljhar on the other, rail tracks are laid. According to area and jurisdiction, the thana and the SDO are given special powers to immediately investigate, take action, prepare cases for court, in instances of atrocities against Adivasis and Harijans. A panchayati well is dug in Dhai village. Dhai is a lower caste and Adivasi village. In this fashion, the area attempts to limp towards modernity.

The result of all this is to make Lachman Singh more powerful. He pooh-poohs government dictates and pays field labourers forty paise as wages, gifts a golden cobra to crown the Shiva idol in Hanuman Misra's temple, buys the BDO a scooter and the daroga a transistor radio, and takes over the bigha and a half of land belonging to Karan and Bulaki as repayment of an old loan.

Everyone accepts all this. But all at once, there is a government circular about field labourers and with it comes a new SDO. This man is suspected of being left-of-centre, and because it is the administration's pious intention to drive the final nail into his coffin and suspend him, he is transferred to Tohri one and a half months before the harvesting season begins.

The field labourers in the Tohri area are Harijans and Adivasis. The landowners, jotedars and mahajans, are upper caste. The particular problem of the area is the deep distrust of the labourers for the masters. This explains the lack of progress in agriculture or increase in individual incomes. Income, expenditure, health, education, social consciousness, everything continues to remain at a sub-normal level. An enlightened, sympathetic, humane officer is needed here.

The SDO realizes that he's in deep trouble. He tells his father-in-law, you win. Look for a bank job for me. I'm a student of Afro-economics, I might even get it. Else, where they're sending me, your only daughter will definitely end up a widow.

Having made alternative job arrangements, the SDO tells the impatient field labourers, 'You have the right to get five rupees eighty paise as wages.' He officially informs the jotedars of this. Lachman Singh's land and crop and labourers are spread over a vast area, including villages like Tamadih, Burudiha, Kuruda, Hesadi, Chama, and Dhai.

The son of the Burudiha village headman, Asrafi Mahato, says, 'We still remember Karan. We haven't forgotten him these three years. But this SDO is a good man. Why should we harvest crops for just forty paise and a meal? Five rupees eighty paise! We don't want the meal, let him give us five rupees forty paise as total wages.'

As he had once explained to Karan, so Dulan now carefully explains to Asrafi, 'Karan made a big noise. As a result, Tamadih's Dusadh quarters went up in flames.'

'Where's Karan? Where's Bulaki?'

'Who knows?'

'They're dead.'

'Why do you say that?'

'They've been killed and buried in the jungle.'

'I don't know. But keep the hakim, the village doctor, with you when you act.'

'All right.'

'Get the hakim to help you later, too. That time, they paid the wages. But later, they lit the fire.'

'I'll tell him.'

In every area, every conflict has a characteristic local pattern.

Lachman Singh says, 'I won't pay that much. Just two rupees and tiffin.'

'Give us the wages, Hujoor, protector.'

'Should I?' Lachman Singh's eyes are terribly gentle and sympathetic. He says, 'Let me think about it! You do the same.'

'Even a donkey knows that those wages are fair. But you know what? You mentioned the SDO, right? Go tell him, in these parts, Makhan Singh, Daitari Singh, Ramlagan Singh, Hujuri Prasad Mahato, no one is giving these wages. Why should I alone be ruined?'

Asrafi offers a timid but stubborn smile, 'Ruined, Hujoor? You own the flour mill, your mansion can be seen from miles away—how can you be ruined?'

To Lachman Singh this smile is arrogant mockery. He says, 'The rate I mentioned is what we decided amongst us. Because we own land, the sarkar treats us like thieves. Yet you get sarkari aid for whatever little land you have. I've given Dulan land. The bastard doesn't farm it, but he collects seeds every year. Animal! He eats them. So let him. And what aid do we get? Fertilizer, seeds, insecticide, we have to buy everything ourselves. Tell the SDO what I said.'

Asrafi tells Dulan, 'Be careful, Chacha! The bastard knows that you don't farm the land or harvest crops.'

The corpses weigh even heavier on Dulan's mind. Lachman Singh has warned him, 'Don't sow or plough the land for a few years, Dulan.'

Dulan, sorrowfully and with deep concern for Asrafi, says, 'Don't trust him, beta. Your father performed the birth rites for my Dhatua-Latua.'

'No, Chacha.'

Asrafi keeps shuttling between the SDO and Lachman Singh. Dulan grows increasingly depressed. Fearing some calamity, he growls at his sons, 'The son of the lowborn will always be lowborn. You eat whatever I manage to wring from the soil. Someone else would have gone off to a nearby colliery. Why are you hanging on here?'

Dhatua raises his calm, dreamy eyes and says, 'This time we'll get double wages, Baba.'

Dulan says nothing further. He goes to the block office at Tohri, says, 'This time I want to sow rabi after the harvest. I need help.'

⌁

The BDO seems to know the irrefutable reason for continuing to supply seeds for land that will never be farmed. He, too, joins Lachman and Dulan in this conspiracy and, smiling toothily, says, 'I'll look into it.'

Dulan notices the huge trees in his compound. Such tall papaya trees are rare.

He says, 'How did this papaya tree grow so tall, Babu?'

The BDO gives a deeply self-satisfied smile, 'This area became a part of the office compound later. During the summer they would shoot mad dogs and dump them in the hole there. Trees are bound to grow well if they're fertilized by rotting bones and flesh.'

'Does it make good fertilizer?'

'Very good. Haven't you seen how flowers flourish on the burial mounds of poor Muslims?'

These words cause the corpses to weigh lighter in Dulan's mind. Returning to his village, Dulan goes to the land in the middle of the afternoon. Yes, true enough! Karan and Bulaki are now those putush bushes and aloe plants! Tears strain at his eyes. 'Karan, you haven't died even in death. But these putush bushes and aloe plants are of no use to anybody, even buffaloes and goats don't eat them. You fought for our rights. Why couldn't you turn into maize or wheat? Or, at the very least, china grass? So we could eat ghato made of the boiled seeds?'

Sorrowing and bitter, he goes to Tamadih. Nobody is around, so he dismantles the fence protecting Lachman Singh's vegetable patch. He rounds up a few buffaloes and clicks his tongue 'Har, har, har' and drives them into the vegetable patch. Then he goes the long way around to the front of the house and says to Lachman Singh, 'Malik, protector, write me a letter. I want admission into hospital. Cough and chest pain.'

'I'll give you the letter after the harvesting.'

'Very good, master.'

Once more, the corpses weigh Dulan down. He returns to the patch of land, digging into the depths of his mind with the pickaxe of anxiety. Tells Karan and Bulaki to move over and make space.

After the harvesting is over? Is someone coming to keep Karan and Bulaki company?

The harvesting is underway. After much debate, two rupees fifty paise a day and a snack are decided upon. Lachman Singh supervises the harvest on horseback. The police ceremonially make an appearance and confirm that the harvesting is peaceful. On the seventh day, everyone gets their wages.

Heaving a sigh of relief, the SDO leaves with the police.

On the eighth day, the storm breaks. Lachman Singh brings in outside labourers to harvest the paddy. Asrafi and the others feel threatened, and, though scared, they speak up stubbornly.

'You can't do this.'

'Who says so? I am doing it. Sons of bitches, see for yourself—I can do it.'

'But—'

'I let you work. I paid you your wages. Bas—the game's over!'

Seeing Asrafi and the others on the verge of creating trouble, the outsiders lower their scythes and huddle together. Shots are fired. The outside labourers flee.

Shots are fired.

There is no account of the number shot dead. According to Dulan and the others, eleven. According to Lachman

Singh and the police, seven. Asrafi's father loses his sons. Two sons, Mohar and Asrafi, both missing. Mahuban Kairi of Chama village and Paras Dhobi of Burudiha—missing. Cries of mourning in almost every home. When the SDO arrives, the fathers, mothers, wives, children of the dead and missing fall at his feet. The SDO's face is as if hewn from rock. He promises the villagers that he'll file a police case against Lachman Singh. He's telling the reporters the whole story, escorting them around. Until the warrant comes, Lachman Singh is not to leave home.

ノ

On a moonlit night, when there's a nip in the sweet-scented air, Lachman Singh arrives. Everything in these areas follows a pattern, and the noblest animal is the four-footed horse.... Four horses carrying four corpses. This time, Lachman's men help Dulan. Deep, deep pits are needed. The land is soaked with monsoon rain and autumn dew. Four corpses piled one on the other. The burden within Dulan grows even heavier.

Dulan becomes increasingly strange. He picks quarrels at the BD office to extract more and more seeds. Money for a plough and buffalo. Then, before the month is out, a few aloe plants bring solace. Very healthy, very green aloe plants and putush bushes accept the salutations of the sun each dawn during the Emergency in neglected southeast Bihar, silent testimony to the murder of field labourers cum Harijans. Lachman is released without being charged. Emergency. The SDO is demoted for undermining the harmony between the labourers and the landowners by inciting the former to revolt.

Lachman and the other Jotedars and mahajans offer puja at Hanuman Misra's temple with savage fanfare and a hundred and eight pure-silver bael leaves, and announce that only those sons and daughters of curs and bitches who are willing to work for one rupee without food or water, need bother to show up. They can bring in outside labour.

The Emergency has caused widespread calamity in the region. Congress musclemen have contracted to get outside labourers. Now the game hots up, becomes even more cruelly entertaining. Four annas out of each days' wages have to be given to the contractor. Whether you are contracted by him or not. These musclemen have vowed that they'll get the crop harvested at gunpoint, and anyone who dares object will be doused in petrol and set on fire, so that matters are settled once and for all.

Dulan wanders around with a heavy mind, and looking at Dhatua-Latua, wonders if they should flee. But where can they go? Where will a Dulan Ganju be safe in his motherland of southeast Bihar?

Is there a place without Lachman Singhs?

During the Holi festival, he doesn't even listen to the songs carefully. But suddenly the joyous celebrations are interrupted by a strange song. Dhatua, intoxicated with mahwa, plays the tuila and sings, his eyes closed:

Where has Karan gone?
And Bulaki?
Why is there no news of them?
They are lost in the police files.
Where is Asrafi Hajam?

And his brother Mohar?
Where are Mahuban and Paras?
Why is there no news of them?
They are lost in the police files.
Karan fought the twenty-five-paise battle.
Asrafi fought the five-rupees-forty-paise battle.
Bulaki and Mohar
Fought alongside their elder brothers.
Mahuban could brew the best mahwa
Paras was the best Holi dancer
All lost in the police files, lost.

The song ends. Everyone is silent. The colours of Holi turn to ash, the intoxication wears off. Dulan stands up.

'Who made up this song?'

'I did, Baba.'

Dulan broke into deep sobs. He said, 'Forget that song. Or you too will get lost in the police files.'

Dulan returned to his land. Climbed down the embankment, into the middle of the patch. In an eerie whisper he said, 'You've become songs. You hear? Songs. Songs made up by my son Dhatua. You've become gaan, song, not dhaan, paddy, not china grass—now get off my chest, I can't take it any more!'

Under the full Holi moon, the fresh leaves of the aloe plants and the rough-barked putush bushes shook with laughter. They had never heard anything so funny. Dulan's heart was filled with an unnamed fear for Dhatua. As soon as he climbed the machan, he heard Dhatua's song. Now everyone was singing it. But they were not lost in the police files. Dulan would never be able to reveal everything. The power of Lachman Singh.

⌇

One day, the Emergency ends.

One day, the Liberation Sun of India gets off the gaddi, her seat of power, to watch the fun, and then, regaining her breath, a little later, begins agitating to regain the gaddi. One day, Lachman Singh's crop ripens, once again.

After two years of drought-famine-crop destruction, this year the earth generously floods the land with paddy. Paddy fields disappearing into the horizon, punctuated with rows of machans. Birds feed on the ripening paddy day and night.

He who was a Congressman and muscleman and field-labour contractor two years ago now expunges the title 'Congress and muscleman' from his name and appears as the Contractor of Field Labour. With him are a Terylene-and-dark-glasses-flaunting, gun-toting foursome, all exactly like him. In an Amitabh Bachchan voice, this mercenary tells Lachman Singh, 'Your days are over. Now, strike-breaking, supplying contract labour, and harvesting is managed by professionals. I provide mercenary services in southeastern Bihar. This service is compulsory. Five thousand bucks. Advance.'

'Five thousand?'

'Are you willing to pay the sarkar's fixed wage rate?'

'No, no.'

'By not paying those rates, you stand to make a profit of eighty thousand. And you don't want to pay five thousand?'

'I'll pay.'

'Bas. Give me the names of the villages and the labourers. Any troublemakers?'

'No.'

'All right. I have to provide services to Ramlagan Singh and Makhan Singh, too. I'll come at the appropriate time. And yes, pay them five sikka as wages. My share is four annas.'

'One rupee.'

'Five sikka. Amarnath Misra doesn't waste words.'

'How are you related to Misraji and Tahar?'

'Bhatija. His brother's son. The seed capital for my services was provided by Chachaji himself.'

Thus everything is settled. Later, Hanuman Misra says to Lachman Singh, 'Yes, yes, he's my bhatija. I bought surface collieries for my sons, and asked him, "Shall I get you one, too?" But no, he didn't want such tiresome work. Very competent and efficient. Election candidates use his services, as do owners of factories on strike. He supplied labour for surface collieries. Very efficient! Three wives. Keeps them in different towns. Built a house for each one. The previous sarkar knew his worth. Not one of my sons turned out as clever as him.'

Lachman Singh, a ruthless Rajput, is all-powerful in his own territory. But even he accepts that this time he has no choice but to accept the services of the mercenaries who are being forced down his throat. If he doesn't, Makhan and Ramlagan will score over him by availing of the services of the gunmen, while his own work will not be done.

Harvesting begins. No outside labourers. Dhatua and the others are doing it themselves. A snack of corn sattu, chilli, salt, and five sikka daily wages. Dhatua's mother packs some pickle of wild karamcha for her two sons to go with the snack.

Dulan sits on the machan. Sits and waits—for what? Harvesting is going on. In the distance, the women are singing as they reap. It sounds like a lullaby. But Dulan can't sleep.

Who has stolen the sleep from Dulan's eyes?
His sleep is lost in the police files.

Dulan waits at home for Dhatua and Latua to return. Then he goes to his land. In the monsoons, wet with showers and the autumn dew, the aloe plants and patush bushes stand arrogant, like a rampant jungle. The bushes are bursting with flowers. Sleep eludes Dulan's eyes.

The expected trouble begins on pay day. Amarnath demands his share. Lachman says, 'No bloodshed, please. You and I have no agreement about cutting your share from the wages. Settle it with them.'

'With all of them?' Amarnath laughs like a hyena. '*You* pay me.'

Dulan's son, Dhatua, resists the most. That's why Lachman Singh doesn't want to get involved. He knows only one way of dealing with the untouchable and that is a bullet from his gun. This is one person he doesn't want to shoot. Dulan is too useful to him.

Amarnath says, 'Talk to these curs? Five sikka for five hundred people. One sikka per day per head works out to one thousand eight hundred seventy-five rupees for fifteen days. Hand it over.'

'No Hujoor! We won't,' Dhatua protests.

Lachman sighs. Once again, he will have to work

according to his usual pattern. Once again he will have to pick up his gun. Karan went, Asrafi came, Asrafi went, now there's Dhatua.

'How can we take home fifteen rupees for fifteen days? Shouldn't we get eighteen rupees twelve annas? Wasn't that agreed upon? We haven't delayed the work, have we?'

'Watch it, Dhatua.'

Lachman Singh hands over the money to Amarnath. Then he says, 'Don't say a word, Dhatua. Just leave.'

Karan was raucous with his demands. Asrafi was aggressive. Dhatua had never known that he could protest so stubbornly over this matter of cutting Amarnath's share from their wages. Stepping out, he tells the others, 'You carry on. I'll settle things before I leave here.'

He returns to face Lachman Singh. Says, 'If you don't settle the account for the remaining twenty-five paise, we won't come to work tomorrow. The best fields are not yet done. We won't work, and we won't let anyone else work, either.'

'You're lucky the police are here for their cut, Dhatua. You're safe this time.'

'Why? Do the police scare you?'

Dhatua leaves, but this last barb enrages Lachman Singh. Even so, since Dhatua is Dulan's son, and Dulan is necessary to his secret, Lachman Singh gives the lower castes a day's time.

The next day, everyone comes, but no one works. Lachman is enraged and frustrated. The mercenaries are not available. They have gone to help Makhan Singh and Ramlagan Singh. Outside labour is not available at short notice. As the light fades into evening, Lachman gives his men the necessary instructions: if threats do the trick, don't open fire. Lachman's men ride their horses through the ripe paddy. Having seen several films on the Chambal dacoit gangs, they too have donned khaki green uniforms. They advance. The other side rises and waits.

'Listen here, you whelps, you sons of bitches!'

'You're the son of a bitch!' Someone shouts.

They raise their guns. This side storms into the field at amazing speed. They vanish into the paddy. First, verbal missiles speed back and forth.

Then the inevitable bullets fly. Lots of them. Flocks of birds leave the ripe paddy and take flight. In the field, someone gargles blood deep in his throat. A familiar sound.

Then, sharp scythes and iron choppers slash the horses' hooves, keep slashing. The horses and their riders thunder on. The others steal out and flee. Latua and Param run off towards Tohri.

A long, long, agonizing wait for Dulan. Evening turns to night, and the night is far gone when Latua returns.

'Where is Dhatua?'

'I haven't seen him. Hasn't he returned? I went to the police thana.'

'Where is Dhatua?'

'We fetched the police. They'll come here as well. The same SDO, Baba. He's back. He'll come too.'

'Dhatua!'

Why are the corpses stirring deep within Dulan? For whom are they making place? For whom? Realization hits Dulan. He starts up.

'Where are you going?'

'To the land.'

'The boy is missing, and you...you...are you mad, or are you a ghost?'

'Shut up, woman.'

Dulan walks out, begins to run. Dhatua's song, Dhatua's song.

Where has Karan gone?
And Bulaki?
They are lost in the police files.

Dreamy eyes. A birthmark on his hand. Don't you get lost, now, Dhatua, don't you get lost. Oh, you aloe plant, you putush bush, don't you laugh at me tonight.

Dhatua is alive, alive.

Lachman Singh. A man. With bloodied face and eyes. Lachman is hitting him. Kicking him. The man falls to the ground.

Two of them, three horses.

Lachman looks at him.

'Come close,' says Dulan.

'Dhatua?'

'Sorry, Dulan, I forbade them, but still these beasts opened fire.'

Lachman kicks the man again. Curses, 'Trigger-happy tough!'

'Dhatua?'

'Buried.'

'Who buried him?'

'This animal.'

'Him?'

71

'Yes. But don't open your mouth, Dulan. Or else your wife, son, son's wife, grandson, no one will be spared. Take, I'll give you money, lots of money. Your son called the police. I'll buy them off, of course. But remember that I'm sparing Latua only because he's your son. I haven't fired a single bullet today. I could have felled Dhatua with a single shot. I didn't.'

They go away. Dulan can no longer stand there with seven corpses. He falls onto the embankment. Rolls down into the field, torn by the savage leaves and thorns of the aloe plants, till he comes to a halt.

As usual, the investigation remains incomplete. The SDO intervenes. The trigger-happy tough and Amarnath go to jail.

Dhatua does not return.

Dulan ponders, on and on. Finally, he decides to go mad. Because he starts uprooting the aloe and putush from his land at the first Baisakhi showers.

'Where's he gone? In the middle of the afternoon?' his wife asks.

Latua's wife says, 'Father-in-law took the scythe and the shovel and went to the field.'

'Why didn't you stop him?'

'Me? Talk to him?!'

All grief forgotten, his wife rushes out. She climbs the embankment and yells, 'Here, have you gone mad? Why are you trying to clear that jungle?'

'Go home.'

'What do you mean, go home?'

'Go home.'

In tears, his wife goes to the pahaan. The pahaan goes to him. Says, 'Dhatua will come back, Dulan. Don't go crazy in despair over your son. Come, you'll fall ill in the heat of the sun.'

Dulan says, 'Go home, pahaan. Is my son missing or is yours?'

'Yours.'

'Is this my land or yours?'

'Yours.'

'Well, then? I may be mad or I may not. What's it to you? I'll fix that bastard's land!'

'Then get Latua to help you.'

'No, I'll do it all alone.'

Though he doesn't farm, he has green fingers, the pahaan remembers. The pahaan tells Dulan's wife, 'Come let's go home. Let him do what he wants. You have to go to Tohri.'

Dulan's wife and Latua visit Tohri repeatedly to enquire at the thana about Dhatua.

For a few days, Dulan clears the undergrowth. Prepares the land. Then he takes the seeds from his house, telling his wife, 'These seeds are not for eating. I'll sow them.'

'On that land!'

'Yes.'

Scattering the seeds on the land, he chants, like a mantra, 'I won't let you be just aloe and putush. I'll turn you into paddy, Dhatua. I'll turn you into paddy.'

When the seedlings appear, everyone comes to see them. Lachman, Makhan, or Ramlagan's fertilizer-fed seedlings are nothing in comparison. These seedlings are as green as they are healthy.

Fallow land, new seedlings. Everyone says so. Dulan, irritated, drives everyone away. He'll do the ploughing and sowing himself, and savour the fresh green by himself.

The pahaan says, 'Lachman Singh would have died of envy if he'd seen this.'

'Who?'

Dulan is indifferent.

'Lachman Singh.'

'Where is he?'

'Gone to Gaya. To his in-laws' place.'

'Oh!'

Then the paddy grows. Tall, strong, healthy plants. A wonderful crop. The paddy ripens. Now Dulan's extreme insanity is revealed.

He says, 'I'm not going to harvest the crop.'

'What? After all the labour of cutting the canal and draining the stagnant water this past monsoon, after staying there day and night, after I wore myself to death carting ghato and water for you each day—you won't reap?'

'No, and no one is to come here. I've work to do.'

'What work? Just sitting?'

'Yes. Just sitting.'

What he was waiting for occurred. Lachman returned for the harvest. The news of Dulan's bumper crop reached him. A year has passed since Dhatua's murder. Lachman is in control of himself again.

Lachman comes to Dulan. Dulan knew he would come. He knew.

'Dulan.'

'Malik, protector?'

'Come here.'

'What's this, you're alone?'

'Don't talk rubbish. What's the meaning of this?'

'What?'

'Why is there paddy on this land?'

'I planted it.'

'What was agreed between us?'

'You tell me.'

'Son of a bitch, didn't I tell you not to farm this land? To leave it as jungle—'

Dulan below, Lachman on horseback. All at once, Dulan grabbed Lachman's foot and pulled hard. Lachman fell. His rifle flew and landed some distance away from him. Then the rifle was in Dulan's hand. Before Lachman could recover his wits, the butt of the rifle slammed into his head. Lachman screamed. Dulan smashed the butt into his collar bone. A snapping sound.

Son of a bitch, bastard.... Frightened, Lachman realized that he was crying before Dulan. Tears of agony and terror. He, Lachman Singh, prostrate on the ground, and Dulan Ganju standing erect? He lunged at Dulan's foot and winced because Dulan had hurled a rock at his outstretched hand. It would be a long time before he could use his right hand again.

'Animal! Cur!'

'What was our agreement, malik? That I shouldn't farm. Why not? You'll sow corpses, and I'll guard them. Why? Otherwise you'll burn down the village, kill my family. Very good. But, malik, seven boys—seven. Is it right for only wild, thorny underbrush to grace their graves? So, I sowed paddy, you see. Everyone says I've gone mad. I have, you know. I won't let you go today, malik, I won't let you harvest your crop. Won't let you shoot, burn houses, kill people. You've harvested enough.'

'Do you think the police will let you go?'

'If they don't, they don't. Your henchmen, too will probably go for me. But when haven't they, malik? Has the police ever let up on us? So they'll beat me—if I die, so be it. Everyone dies sometime. Did Dhatua die before his time?'

Knowing that he was helpless, Lachman Singh was filled with the fear of death. But even in the throes of this fear, in southeast Bihar, the Rajput will never beg the lowborn for mercy. Even if he did, the lowborn will not always be able to gift him his life. As Dulan could not.

As Lachman tried his best to stand up, shout, or lift a stone with his left hand, Dulan said, 'What a pity, malik! You had to die by a Ganju's hand!'

He began to smash Lachman's head with a rock. Over and over again. Lachman a professional killer, knew the value of a bullet, so murder was no cause for disturbance. He would have killed Dulan with a single bullet.

Dulan is not used to killing, a rock has no value, this death is the result of years of intense mental turmoil. He continued to smash Lachman's head in till he knew he could stop.

Dulan stood up. There were many things to be done, one by one. He led the horse forward by the reins, brought a stick down on its haunches and drove it off. Let it go where it will. He lashed Lachman, gun and all, with a rope, dragged him away and dumped him in a ditch. Then he rolled stone after stone into it. Stone after stone. Laughter begins to well up inside him. So, malik, protector, you're like the disgusting Oraon Munda? Buried under stones? A stony grave?

No telltale signs were likely to remain on the hard, rocky ground. But he broke off a leafy branch from a nearby putush bush to sweep away any marks of a struggle. Then he climbed onto the machan.

The search for Lachman continued for a few days. Since he never consulted anyone, Lachman had not mentioned that he was going to see Dulan. This was only natural, since his dependence on Dulan had to be kept secret. Those of his henchmen who knew kept their mouths shut. When the malik protector himself goes missing, when his horse is discovered grazing on Daitari Singh's land, why irritate a fresh wound? Lachman's servant said, 'He drank his sweetened milk as usual, and rode off. How do I know where he went?'

A very strange business. Only when the hyenas began to howl did people begin to get suspicious. That too, five days later. For five days, the scavengers, smelling flesh beneath the stones, howled, and with great effort shifted the stones, but managed to devour only the face. The strategic cunning with which the corpse was concealed, plus the presence of the horse in his fields, led to Daitari being suspected. Lachman's son supported this view and, because of an old history of feuds, Daitari was questioned for a few days. Then the police gave up for lack of evidence, though Lachman's son and Daitari continued the old tradition of conflict. At no stage did any suspicion touch Dulan. It was natural not to suspect him. Impossible to imagine Dulan killing Lachman, whatever the circumstances.

✧

On the one hand, Lachman-related investigations continue, on the other, a new, contented Dulan descends from the machan. He speaks to the pahaan, and as a result, all of

Kuruda village gathers in the pahaan's courtyard one evening.

Dulan says, 'I've never given anyone anything, ever.'

Everyone is stunned.

'All of you praised my crop. When I didn't harvest it, you said I was mad. While I was farming, you called me mad. You called this fool a fool. Now listen to what this madman has to say.'

'Go ahead!'

There is a sense of relief after Lachman's death. Right now, no one wants to worry about the son taking on the father's role.

'My paddy is your seed. Take it.'

'You're giving it away?'

'Yes, take it, reap it. There's a long story behind this—did I use fertilizer? Yes I did, very precious fertilizer.' Dulan's voice disappears like the string of a severed kite losing itself in the sky. Then, clearing his throat he says, 'You harvest it. Give me some, as well, I'll sow it again and again.'

After they promise that they will harvest the crop when the time came, Dulan returns to his land. His heart is strangely, wonderfully light today! He stands on the embankment and looks at the paddy.

Karan, Asrafi, Mohar, Bulaki, Mahuban, Paras, and Dhatua—what amazing joy there is in the ripe, green paddy nourished on your flesh and bones! Because you will be seed. To be a seed is to stay alive. Slowly, Dulan climbs up to the machan. A tune in his heart. Dhatua made up this song. Dhatua, Dulan's voice trembles as he says the name. Dhatua, I've turned you all into seed.

COINSANV'S CATTLE

Damodar Mauzo

TRANSLATED FROM THE KONKANI BY XAVIER COTA

Driving his cattle before him, Inas herded them into the shed where he tethered them for the night before entering the house through the back door. Bent over the fireplace, Coinsanv was coaxing the fire to life by patiently blowing on the embers. Hearing Inas come in, she asked in surprise, 'Haven't you tied the cows yet, Inas?'

'I've just come in after tying them,' mumbled Inas, sitting down on the box by the wall. Retrieving the butt of the viddi stuck above his ear, he struck a match to it and drew in the smoke, deeply.

'Strange! Then, why aren't they lowing today?' Coinsanv asked in wonder. Invariably, the cows would set off a continuous mooing after being tied up in the shed. And here was Inas, back in the house after tying them and they were still silent!

'They dare not open their mouths!'

'Why? What happened?' Coinsanv asked with a stab of apprehension. 'Did they enter someone's garden or....'

'Not in anybody's garden. They got into Paulu Bhatkar's coconut grove. They chewed some of his saplings, it seems. He threatened to impound them unless I paid him fifteen rupees. Only after I pleaded with him and promised to work on his plot did he let them go.'

Coinsanv heard him out in silence. Warming the tea that she'd brewed in the afternoon, she poured out a mug and placed it in front of Inas. The cattle were still quiet.

'Bitter...like poison!' muttered Inas, grimacing distastefully after taking a sip of the smoky, stale black tea.

But Coinsanv was too preoccupied to pay attention to his grumbling. Why are the cattle still not mooing? How could they still not be hungry!

'Did the cows destroy many coconut saplings?'

'Nonsense! Not a single one! I doubt that they even touched a single leaf!' In that case.... In a trice Coinsanv realized what had happened. 'Inas, did you by chance vent your anger with the landlord on the cows?'

Inas's sullen silence was answer enough.

Leaving whatever she was doing, Coinsanv rushed to the cowshed. Both the cow and the bull were standing mutely. Normally, they would both lick her with their sandpaper-like tongues as soon as she walked into the shed. Today, they made no such move. For a moment, Coinsanv imagined that they were averting their gaze from her! Could they be angry? Coinsanv laid both her hands on each of their backs. Immediately, they both started trembling. The cow started mooing first, followed immediately by the bull. Coinsanv started stroking the cow's neck with one hand and, with the other, she gently scratched the bull's forehead. The cow responded by licking her hand. Coinsanv's glance roved over the animals minutely. Though there were no definite welts on their bodies, Coinsanv's experienced eyes could tell exactly where each stroke of the lash had landed. The animals were now continuously lowing in unison. They were famished.

Patting them, Coinsanv coaxed them gently, 'Okay, okay, quiet now.' She then went to the house. Inas was outside readying the coconut fronds for thatching.

'Inas, is there any oilcake in the house?'

Inas maintained a stoic silence. In any case, what could he do? Whose stomach was he supposed to fill? Three children. With their precarious hand-to-mouth existence, all they could think about was getting through each day. As long as the cow was yielding milk, they could afford to buy oilcake. Last year they had a pair of bullocks which they used for ploughing. But at Christmas, the black bull had died. Had it not died, they would have earned something from ploughing. Now, how could they afford oilcake for a cow gone dry and an idle bull?

'There's a little bran in the house, Inas. I'll go and collect some dhonn. Don't go out.'

By the time she made the rounds of their four Hindu neighbours, collecting the slop that they kept for her, the Angelus bells were ringing. She had barely entered the house, balancing the earthen pot on her head, when the cows set off an insistent bellowing.

Lowering the pot, Coinsanv put her hand in a bag and drew out some bran that she'd saved. She distributed the bran equally between two kodhim. Pouring the slop into both the earthen vessels, she stirred it with her hand till the bran was soaked.

The cattle were still lowing ceaselessly. Inas came out. Flicking the butt of his viddi, he got to work. Taking an old broom, he quickly cleared away the area in front of the cows. As soon as Coinsanv had finished stirring, he lifted the feed containers and placed them in front of the cattle. They began to feed greedily. Coinsanv went to the well and drew a pitcher of water. By this time, the cattle had licked the containers dry. Pouring water into them, Coinsanv went inside. Outside, the children could be heard raising a ruckus. The pot was bubbling on the fire. Inas must have kept the rice water to boil while she'd gone to collect the slop. Mentally thanking him for his thoughtfulness, Coinsanv resumed her interrupted chores.

She roasted some dried sardines on the embers. After removing them from the coals, she sprinkled the last few drops of coconut oil from the bottle. The aroma that wafted up was appetizing.

'O, Inas!' somebody from outside called out.

'Coming!' Inas replied from the back as Pedru made himself comfortable on the balcão. Catching a whiff of the roasted salt fish, he joked, 'Coinsanv, I'm inviting myself to dinner tonight!'

'Please join us! We have excellent fish today!' retorted Coinsanv.

'That's obvious from the aroma!' Pedru laughed, lighting up a viddi. By then Inas came out.

'Where are the cattle, Inas?' Pedru's question made Coinsanv's heart skip a beat. What now? Had their cattle got into somebody else's compound too? Pedru's next remark allayed the fear.

'Day after tomorrow is the Purument fest in Margao. I'll be taking my buffalo heifer to sell at the fair. I've come to see if you're planning to go too.'

After a moment's hesitation, Inas replied, 'No. You carry on.'

His logic was telling him to sell the cattle. A single bull was useless for ploughing and a cow that yielded no milk was expensive to look after. But his prudence was warning him not to do anything without consulting Coinsanv. She loved the animals dearly.

'Don't be foolish! Your bull is getting old. What will you do if he too dies?' asked Pedru, exhaling smoke.

Inas remained quiet. Inside, Coinsanv listened intently. Pedru continued, 'I'm selling my heifer. If I get a good crop this year, I may buy another one next year. You decide about yours. But do remember that you'll get the best price only at this fair. In my opinion, you'd better sell both the cow and the bull. You can always buy one later.'

Pedru left, yet Inas did not go back in. Coinsanv must have heard every word that Pedru spoke. But he did not dare broach the subject with her. Coinsanv called the children in to eat. She served them bits of the roasted salt fish along with the kanji.

'Coinsanv, I'll be back soon,' said Inas.

Coinsanv knew exactly where Inas had gone.

Reflecting on what Pedru had said, Coinsanv squatted in front of the fireplace. One cow and a pair of bulls. How Coinsanv had doted on them! There was nothing that both she and Inas wouldn't do for them. They had even deprived themselves to feed the cattle. Despite this, one bull had died of snakebite exactly on Christmas Day. During Carnival, the cow had stopped yielding milk. And now....

When fending for three children and two adults was itself an overwhelming task, can one afford to be emotional about animals? The spiralling prices.... They were already in the last days of May and had not even thought about the transplanting of paddy which had to be done before the monsoon broke out in June. Others had already germinated their seedlings. Some had already been transplanted, hoping for early rains. Both Coinsanv's paddy plots were still fallow.

The neighbours kept asking her, 'When will you be sowing?' But where would she get so much money from? Seedlings, fertilizer, weeding—for all this she needed...yes. It was essential that they sowed their field. It was only because they had cultivated last year that their children could at least have kanji this year. Otherwise they would...! They must sow...the rains were nearing...day after tomorrow was the Pentecost fair where one had to stock up on provisions for the rainy season!

Inas trooped in after a tot at the taverna. Coinsanv served Inas some kanji. Inas glanced into the kanji buddkulo. As Coinsanv readied to ladle out some more for him, Inas said he'd had enough. Coinsanv guessed that he'd said that because there was very little kanji left in the pot. But Coinsanv was not hungry and said, 'I've already eaten, Inas. You eat well. You have to work tomorrow.'

'Don't lie to me. Have that kanji!' said Inas, getting up.

Coinsanv sipped her rice gruel and got up. She cleaned up the fireplace and came out of the kitchen. The kids were fast asleep. Inas had squatted on the box and was puffing away.

'Inas, day after tomorrow is the Purument feast.'

Inas dragged on the viddi and exhaled, but remained silent. He was bothered by the same thoughts.

'You're taking the cattle, aren't you?'

Inas stiffened. Was Coinsanv goading him? Testing him? Inas shook his head vigorously.

'What do you mean by no? Are you mad?' She was speaking to Inas but was obviously trying to convince herself. 'How will we manage if we don't sell the cattle? Don't we have to sow the fields? Where will the money for the fertilizer, the seedlings, come from? From your father?'

Inas heard Coinsanv out in wonder. He had been thinking along the same lines but hadn't said anything because of Coinsanv's feelings. Now Coinsanv was herself telling him this!

'Are you serious?' Inas croaked in disbelief.

'Is this the time for jokes? There's only tomorrow. On the day after, you take them at dawn. Do you want me to come along?'

'There's no need.' Inas was relieved. All along, he'd been hesitating to broach the subject but now Coinsanv was herself urging him to sell the cattle. He slept soundly. After Coinsanv blew out the light and went to bed, Inas wasn't awake to hear her sobbing bitterly.

Getting through the next day was hell. Early in the morning, Mari-Santan called out, 'Coinsanv, have you seen the sky? It looks like the monsoon is coming soon!'

'Maybe.'

'Aren't you transplanting?'

'We're transplanting after the feast.'

'You'd better hurry up! The rains are around the corner! Some people have already transplanted. And haven't you heard, people are queuing up for fertilizer? You better reserve yours fast!'

If in the morning it was Mari-Santan, Caitan came by at noon. 'Have you bought your paddy seedlings?'

'Not yet.'

'Do you want some?' Caitan asked.

'Do you have stock?'

'Not me. But Bebdo-Santan, the drunkard, has some for sale. If you need it, you better tell him now.'

'I'll speak to Inas about it.'

The cows had not been put out to pasture that morning. Coinsanv herself took them to graze in the evening. Taking out some money that she'd saved, she bought a kilo of oilcake. Earlier, with one rupee you could get a kilo of oilcake and a small tablet of bathing soap besides. Now soap has become precious and a rupee would not even buy a kilo of oilcake! Mentally cursing the greedy shopkeeper, Coinsanv soaked the cake in water. Asking Inas to remain in the house, she went to the houses of the neighbouring Hindus. At each house, she collected the slop and, barely controlling the tears welling up in her eyes, she told them, 'From tomorrow, we won't need the slop. We are selling the cattle in the morning!'

Ladling out a generous portion of feed for the cattle, Inas and Coinsanv went in. Both were heavy-hearted. They had brought up these two dumb animals like their own children. And now they had to sell them for the sake of their own stomachs.

It was a terrible night, full of turmoil for them both.

Coinsanv got up at the crack of dawn. She lit the fire and put the kettle on for tea. She went into the cowshed and sitting with the animals, she cried her heart out. She got up when she sensed that Inas had woken up. Coinsanv poured out the tea and both of them sipped it in silence by the fireplace. Outside, the world was stirring. Filip, Hari, and Pedru were supposed to be taking their cattle for the fair. As he was putting on his shirt, Inas told her, 'Coinsanv, go to our field and straighten out the ridges. And send a message to Bebdo-Santan that we'll need his seedlings. If it rains tomorrow, we can transplant the day after.' But Coinsanv was hardly listening. Her other ear was in the cowshed.

Pedru arrived noisily. 'Hoi there, Inas!'

Inas went out through the back door, untied the animals, and herded them out of the shed. Coinsanv couldn't restrain herself. Rushing out of the house, she hugged the cow. The bull came up to her and started licking her calves. With that, the dam burst and Coinsanv cried a flood of tears.

'You get inside now!' muttered Inas gruffly.

Her leaden feet would not move and Coinsanv remained rooted to the spot she was standing upon. Inas tugged at the cattle. Since Pedru was almost out of sight, he stepped up his pace, straining at the ropes. Coinsanv sensed that the cow's feet had become heavy and the cattle didn't want to go. Inas was actually having to drag them away. What Coinsanv wanted to say was, 'No, Inas! Don't take them!' but the words did not come. What broke out instead were uncontrollable sobs. She sank down to the ground and squatted on her heels.

As the sun came out brightly, Coinsanv got a grip on herself. It was over. She served breakfast to the children and went to the fields. With a hoe, she softened the soil and levelled it. She then straightened the ridges. Having spent half a day there, she went home. After lunch, she went to Santan's and booked some seedlings. She next went to the fertilizer shop and found out which was ideal. 'I'll collect it tomorrow, keep some for me,' she told the shopkeeper. When she reached home again, she remembered her cows. She became uneasy. Her feet took her to the cowshed. She entered the shed; its emptiness oppressed her. Such wonderful animals! We should never have sold them. Where did we get this awful idea? Our cattle were so loving, so gentle. If that stupid Pedru weren't to come that day, we wouldn't even have thought of it! Hurling two curses at Pedru, a couple at Inas, and cursing herself, too, Coinsanv got up. She then put rice in the pot boiling on the fire for kanji. As she put it in, she consoled herself. Never mind; let the cattle go! At least we won't go hungry next year. The sun had set and the lengthening shadows of darkness were casting their gloom in the house. Misgivings started assailing Coinsanv once again. It was this same cow's milk that nourished my children. By selling her milk, we could manage to buy provisions. This very bull helped maintain our household with his ploughing. And today we have decided to sell them! Our lovely cattle! God help us! I hope nobody buys our cow! I hope our bull comes back! Coinsanv consoled herself with these fervent pleas.

It was past Angelus, time for Inas to be back. But Coinsanv did not allow herself to go out and sit. Without even lighting a lamp, she squatted inside in the dark.

Quite often, many cattle come back unsold. But those cattle are quite different. Our animals are so loving; anybody will grab them. We should never have sent them! As she sat there with these thoughts tormenting her, she heard the distant tinkling of cowbells. Coinsanv stepped out.

Pedru was in front. Inas was trailing him. In the darkness

she felt she could make out Pedru returning with his buffalo. But she had forgotten that Pedru's buffalo did not have a bell. Surmising that Coinsanv would be pleased even if the cows were not sold, Inas was coming back with the cows with a spring in his step.

A stunned Coinsanv was motionless for a moment. That fallow field, those seedlings, that fertilizer—everything began swimming before her eyes. The cow had barely started licking her hand affectionately when Coinsanv began screaming and flailing her arms at the two dumb animals. 'You whore! You wretched animals! How the hell are we to manage now? How are we to sow the field? What are we going to eat next year? Go—and die!'

THE HANGING

O. V. Vijayan

TRANSLATED FROM THE MALAYALAM BY A. J. THOMAS

Vellaayiappan set out for Kannur. As he began his journey, a wailing rose from the family members gathered in his hut and from Ammini's hut. The fifty or so families in the village of Paazhuthara listened to the mournful sounds and grieved along with the mourners. If they had had the funds to accompany Vellaayiappan, Ammini and the rest of the villagers would have gone with him to Kannur. But the villagers were so poverty stricken that Vellaayiappan made the journey alone.

He left the last of the huts of the village behind and took the earthen bund that led across the paddy fields. Behind him, the lament of the villagers grew faint as he walked on. The bund he was walking on led to a footpath that meandered through pasture land.

'My gods, my lords,' Vellaayiappan wept within himself.

The footpath was lined with palmyra palms on both sides. A strong wind rattled the fronds of the palms. Today, the familiar sound seemed strange, it was as if the gods and ancestors were communing with him. As he walked on, he felt the dampness of the cooked rice his wife had wrapped for him in a piece of cloth begin to soak his arm. The tears of his wife, Kodachi, as she cooked the rice, must have seeped into the sour curd that it was mixed with, he thought; it was the wetness of tears that was dripping on his arm.

The railway station was four miles away. As he walked towards it, he saw Kuttihassan approaching. Kuttihassan reverentially stepped aside as he came up to him.

'Vellaayi,' said Kuttihassan.

'Kuttihassan,' said Vellaayiappan.

Just two words. Nothing more. Yet both the travellers could sense the strings of sentiments and unspoken sentences that lay beneath the surface.

An unvoiced conversation passed between them:

'Kuttihassan, I am yet to return the fifteen rupees I borrowed from you.'
'Vellaayi, you shouldn't be thinking about this matter today.'
'Kuttihassan, it's just that I might never be able to repay you.'
'Unpaid debts are for the Creator to keep. Let it remain that way.'
'I am burning inside. I feel my life force is being drained away.'
'May God keep you, may His beloved Prophet comfort you, may your gods and mine help you.'

Vellaayiappan continued his journey. The wind in the palmyra fronds turned dense with intense intimations of the deities. Soon he encountered another acquaintance, Neeli, the washerwoman, carrying her bundles of freshly washed clothes. She too stepped aside from the path.

'Vellaayiappan.'

'Neeli.'

Just two words once again. But, as before, they contained a torrent of unsaid things.

Vellaayiappan walked on. The path widened into a dirt road that eventually came to a river. On the other side of the river was an embankment, and beyond it, the road that led to the railway station. Vellaayiappan waded into the shallows of the river. Schools of fish nibbled at his calves. He walked deeper into the waters. Memories arose within him—bathing his father's corpse, teaching his young son how to swim. The memories overwhelmed him, and once he'd crossed the river, Vellaayiappan sank down to the riverbank and wept.

Presently, he picked himself up and continued towards the station, although tears continued to trickle down his face. When he got to the station, Vellaayiappan stood in line to buy a ticket. The train fare was knotted up in a corner of his mundu. When his turn came, he said 'Kannur' to the ticket clerk. The clerk gave him his ticket, and as he did so, Vellaayiappan thought: the first stage of my journey is over.

Carefully tying the ticket into a knot in his mundu, Vellaayiappan made his way to the platform and sat down on a bench to wait for his train. Over the darkening palmyra trees in the distance, birds were returning to their nests. Vellaayiappan remembered how, as a little boy, his son would look in wonderment at the birds returning to their nests at dusk, as they walked through the paddy fields. Then he thought of walking with his own father in the gathering dark through the paddy fields, holding on to his hand with his little finger just as his son had done. Two pictures in his memory, and between them an ocean of unexpressed things.

An old man came to sit beside him on the bench.

'Going to Coimbatore?'

'To Kannur,' Vellaayiappan replied.

'I'm off to Coimbatore,' the other said.

'I see,' Vellaayiappan said.

'The Kannur train will arrive at ten o'clock.'

'I see,' Vellaayiappan said.

'What are going to Kannur for?'

'Nothing in particular.'

'Oh, just for fun, then.'

The stranger's conversation began to grate, his words began to wind themselves around his neck like a noose. He thought, once you leave the paddy fields of Paazhuthara behind, you enter a world of strangers, and their uncaring, impersonal conversations form countless nooses around your neck.

The Coimbatore train arrived and the old man got up and left, leaving Vellaayiappan on his own once again. He did not feel like eating the rice his wife had packed. He could feel its wetness through the cloth in which it was packed. He dozed off and dreamed unquiet dreams. He called out in his sleep, 'O, my son, Kandunni.'

The hissing of steam and the rumbling of the tracks woke him from his sleep. His train had arrived. Vellaayiappan got up from the bench, checked that his ticket was still securely knotted into his mundu, picked up his packed rice, and walked down the platform looking for a compartment he could get into. He was turned away from the first one he tried.

'This is the first-class compartment, O elder.'

'Oh? Is that so?' He walked further down the train.

'This is a reserved compartment.'

'Oh, really.'

'Try elsewhere, O venerable one.'

The voices of strangers.

Vellaayiappan finally managed to climb into a crowded carriage. There was no space to sit but he mused to himself: 'I'll stand, I don't need to sleep. My son is certainly not going to sleep tonight.'

The changing terrain caused the train's rhythm to change every moment; he noted the trackside lamps flashing past, the dim contours of the riverbank, trees, other objects vaguely glimpsed. He had travelled by train just once before, many years ago. That journey had taken place in daylight, this was a night train. They were passing through a long tunnel, on the walls of which there was fading graffiti.

It was not yet daybreak when they reached Kannur. He still hadn't opened the parcel of curd rice his wife had packed for him. Getting off the train, Vellaayiappan made his way out of the station; he handed over his ticket to the ticket collector at the gate. In the far reaches of the darkness above him, there were signs of the coming dawn. The tonga drivers clustered around the station did not pester him.

He asked one of them, 'Which way is the jail?'

Another driver laughed: 'Look at this old man enquiring about the way to the jail so early in the morning.'

A driver standing nearby sniggered and said: 'Eh, old man, just steal something. Best way to land in jail.'

The voices of these strangers wrapped themselves around his throat and began strangling him. Vellaayiappan felt asphyxiated.

Finally, someone took pity on him and pointed him in the direction of the jail. Vellaayiappan began to walk towards it. The skies above him slowly began to lighten; the cawing of crows filled the air.

At the gates of the jail, Vellaayiappan was stopped by a sentry.

'What are you doing here so early in the morning?'

Vellaayiappan felt so helpless, he was on the point of breaking down. Then he slowly unknotted a portion of the mundu tied around his waist, and took out a crumpled, yellowing piece of paper.

'What's this?'

Vellaayiappan handed over the piece of paper to the sentry, who cast a cursory glance at it.

Vellaayiappan then said, 'My child is here.'

The sentry said gruffly: 'Who asked you to come so early? Let the office open.' The man then looked down again at the piece of paper he held in his hand, and registered what was written on it. All at once, his face softened, grew compassionate.

'It's taking place tomorrow, isn't it?'

'I don't really know,' Vellaayiappan replied. 'What's written on the paper?'

The guard looked closely at the document in his hand and then said, 'Yes, at five in the morning.'

Vellaayiappan's face filled with sorrow.

'Please sit down, sir,' the guard said, pointing to the steps leading up to the gates of the jail. Wearily, Vellaayiappan slumped on to a step looking like someone waiting for the sanctum of a temple to open and admit him.

'May I get you some tea, O elder?' the guard asked him. 'No.'

Vellaayiappan thought: 'My son would have remained sleepless all night. If he hasn't slept, how is he going to awaken, break his fast?' His hand reached down to the bundle of rice he had brought with him. 'Son, your mother packed this rice for me. I haven't eaten it. This is all I have to give you.' The heat had turned the rice rancid.

The sky began to brighten, the day grew hotter.

The jail office opened, employees took their places behind desks. The guards took part in the morning parade. There was activity everywhere. Officers shouted orders, sentries checked papers. All these voices twined together to form impersonal nooses that wound themselves around Vellaayiappan, suffocating him. The day grew even hotter. Still, he waited.

Eventually, the guard led him into the prison, down cool corridors that had never known the heat of the sun.

'Here.'

Kandunni stood before him, behinds the bars of a locked cell. His son looked at him without emotion as if he were a stranger, his mind seemed incapable of giving or receiving consolation. The guard unlocked the door and let Vellaayiappan into the cell. For some moments, father and son faced each other, motionless, without a sound. Then Vellaayiappan embraced his son. Kandunni wailed in terror and pain, a sound almost beyond the range of hearing. Weeping, Vellaayiappan said brokenly, 'My son.'

Kandunni said, 'Appa.'

Just those words. Yet what lay between them was the enormity of sorrow and unexpressed words:

'Son, what did you do?'
'I don't remember, Appa.'
'Son, did you murder anyone?'
'I don't remember.'
'It's all right, son. You don't have to remember anything any more.'
'Will the guards remember?'
'No, my son.'
'Will you remember my pain, Appa?'

Again an intense keening issued from Kandunni, a wail so high-pitched and shrill, it was on the edge of auditory perception.

'Appa, don't let them hang me.'

'Time's up, sir. Please come out.'

Vellaayiappan walked out of the cell and the door clanged shut. When he looked back, he saw his son looking at him from behind the bars as a stranger might from behind the barred window of a train hurtling past.

Vellaayiappan kept walking. Just before he turned the bend in the corridor, he looked back one last time, to bid his son farewell.

For the rest of the day, he wandered listlessly around the jail compound, keeping a sort of vigil for his son. The sun rose higher and then the day began to ebb away. When night fell, Vellaayiappan wondered whether his son would sleep that night. When dawn broke, Kandunni was still alive within the walls of the jail.

Vellaayiappan heard the sound of bugles at dawn. He wasn't aware that they signalled the start of the execution.

The sentry had told him that the hanging would take place at five in the morning. Vellaayiappan had no wrist watch but his peasant's instincts told him what time it was.

ᔕ

When the guards delivered his son's body to him, Vellaayiappan received it as a midwife would a baby.

'O, elder, what funeral ceremony did you have in mind for your son?'

'I don't know.'

'Don't you want the body?'

'Masters, I have no money.'

The prison officials handed the body over to the scavengers who took care of such things and instructed them to transport the body to the public burial ground. The scavengers put the body on a trolley and began pushing it towards the cemetery. Vellaayiappan walked along with them. On the outskirts of town, a place of desolate marshes; vultures wheeled in the sky above them.

When they got to the burial ground, the scavengers dug a pit and laid the body in it. Just before they closed the grave Vellaayiappan looked at his son's face one last time. He placed his hand on his cold forehead in a final blessing.

After the scavengers had filled in the grave, Vellaayiappan walked aimlessly away from the burial ground in the intense heat of the day. Eventually, his wanderings brought him to the seashore. He was seeing the sea for the first time. He became aware of something cold and wet in his hands, and realized he was still carrying the rice his wife had prepared for his journey. Vellaayiappan opened the bundle and scattered the rice on the ground in remembrance of his dead son. From the gleaming sunlit dome of the sky, crows descended on the sacrificial rice—like embodied spirits of the dead come to receive the offering.

NON-FICTION

MY IDEA OF VILLAGE SWARAJ

Mohandas Karamchand Gandhi

26 July 1942

My idea of Village Swaraj is that it is a complete republic, independent of its neighbours for its wants, and yet interdependent for many others in which dependence is a necessity. Thus every village's first concern will be to grow its own food crops and cotton for its cloth. It should have a reserve for its cattle, recreation and playground for adults and children. Then if there is more land available, it will grow useful money crops, thus excluding ganja, tobacco, opium, and the like. The village will maintain a village theatre, school, and public hall. It will have its own waterworks ensuring clean supply. This can be done through controlled wells and tanks. Education will be compulsory up to the final basic course. As far as possible every activity will be conducted on the cooperative basis. There will be no castes such as we have today with their graded untouchability. Non-violence with its technique of satyagraha and non-cooperation will be the sanction of the village community. There will be a compulsory service of village guards who will be selected by rotation from the register maintained by the village. The government of the village will be conducted by the panchayat of five persons, annually elected by the adult villagers, male and female, possessing minimum prescribed qualifications. These will have all the authority and jurisdiction required. Since there will be no system of punishments in the accepted sense, this panchayat will be the legislature, judiciary, and executive combined to operate for its year of office. Any village can become such a republic today without much interference, even from the present government whose sole effective connection with the villages is the exaction of the village revenue. I have not examined here the question of relations with the neighbouring villages and the centre if any. My purpose is to present an outline of village government. Here there is perfect democracy based upon individual freedom. The individual is the architect of his own government. The law of non-violence rules him and his government. He and his village are able to defy the might of a world. For the law governing every villager is that he will suffer death in the defence of his and his village's honour....

The reader may well ask me—I am asking myself while penning these lines—as to why I have not been able to model Sevagram after the picture here drawn. My answer is: I am making the attempt. I can see dim traces of success though I can show nothing visible. But there is nothing inherently impossible in the picture drawn here. To model such a village may be the work of a lifetime. Any lover of true democracy and village life can take up a village, treat it as his world and sole work, and he will find good results.

1 January 1937

An ideal Indian village will be so constructed as to lend itself to perfect sanitation. It will have cottages with sufficient light and ventilation built of a material obtainable within a radius of five miles of it. The cottages will have courtyards enabling householders to plant vegetables for domestic use and to house their cattle. The village lanes and streets will be free of all avoidable dust. It will have wells according to its needs and accessible to all. It will have houses of worship for all, also a common meeting place, a village common for grazing its cattle, a cooperative dairy, primary and secondary schools in which industrial education will be the central fact, and it will have panchayats for settling disputes. It will produce its own grains, vegetables and fruit, and its own khadi. This is roughly my idea of a model village. In the present circumstances its cottages will remain what they are with slight improvements. Given a good zamindar, where there is one, or cooperation among the people, almost the whole of the programme other than model cottages can be worked out at expenditure within means of the villagers including the zamindar or zamindars, without government assistance. With that assistance there is no limit to the possibility of village reconstruction. But my task just now is to discover what the villagers can do to help themselves if they have mutual cooperation and contribute voluntary labour for the common good. I am convinced that they can, under intelligent guidance, double the village income as distinguished from individual income. There are in our villages inexhaustible resources not for commercial purposes in every case but certainly for local purposes in almost every case. The greatest tragedy is the hopeless unwillingness of the villagers to better their lot.

The very first problem the village worker will solve is its sanitation. It is the most neglected of all the problems that baffle workers and that undermine physical well-being and breed disease. If the worker became a voluntary Bhangi, he would begin by collecting night-soil and turning it into manure and sweeping village streets. He will tell people how and where they should perform daily functions and speak to them on the value of sanitation and the great injury caused by its neglect. The worker will continue to do the work whether the villagers listen to him or no.

8 February 1935

The things to attend to in the villages are cleaning tanks and wells and keeping them clean, getting rid of dung-heaps. If the workers will begin the work themselves, working like paid Bhangis from day to day and always letting the villagers know that they are expected to join them so as ultimately to do the whole work themselves, they may be sure that they will find that the villagers will sooner or later cooperate.

Lanes and streets have to be cleansed of all the rubbish, which should be classified. There are portions which can be turned into manure, portions which have simply to be buried and portions which can be directly turned into wealth. Every bone picked up is valuable raw material from which useful articles can be made or which can be crushed into rich manure. Rags and waste paper can be turned into paper and excreta picked up are golden manure for the village fields. The way to treat the excreta is to mix them, liquid as well as solid, with superficial earth in soil dug no deeper than one foot at the most. In his book on rural hygiene, Dr Poore says that excreta should be buried in earth no deeper than 9–12 inches (I am quoting from memory). The author contends that superficial earth is charged with minute life, which, together with light and air which easily penetrate it, turn the excreta into good soft sweet-smelling soil within a week. Any villager can test this for himself. The way to do it is either to have fixed latrines, with earthen or iron buckets, and empty the contents in properly prepared places from day to day, or to perform the function directly on to the ground dug up in squares. The excreta can either be buried in a village common or in individual fields. This can only be done by the cooperation of the villagers. At the worst, an enterprising villager can collect the excreta and turn them into wealth for himself. At present, this rich manure, valued at lakhs of rupees, runs to waste every day, fouls the air and brings disease into the bargain.

Village tanks are promiscuously used for bathing, washing clothes, and drinking and cooking purposes. Many village tanks are also used by cattle. Buffaloes are often to be seen wallowing in them. The wonder is that, in spite of this sinful misuse of village tanks, villages have not been destroyed by epidemics. It is the universal medical evidence that this neglect to ensure purity of the water supply of villages is responsible for many of the diseases suffered by the villagers.

This, it will be admitted, is a gloriously interesting and instructive service, fraught with incalculable benefit to the suffering humanity of India. I hope it is clear from my description of the way in which the problem should be tackled, that, given willing workers who will wield the broom and the shovel with the same ease and pride as the pen and the pencil, the question of expense is almost wholly eliminated. All the outlay that will be required is confined to a broom, a basket, a shovel and pickaxe, and possibly some disinfectant. Dry ashes are, perhaps, as effective a disinfectant as any that a chemist can supply. But here let philanthropic chemists tell us what is the most effective and cheap village disinfectant that villagers can improvise in their villages.

18 August 1940

If rural reconstruction were not to include rural sanitation, our villages would remain the muckheaps that they are today. Village sanitation is a vital part of village life and is as difficult as it is important. It needs a heroic effort to eradicate age-long insanitation. The village worker who is ignorant of the science of village sanitation, who is not a successful scavenger, cannot fit himself for village service.

It seems to be generally admitted that without the new or basic education the education of millions of children in India is well-nigh impossible. The village worker has, therefore, to master it and become a basic education teacher himself.

Adult education will follow in the wake of basic education as a matter of course. Where this new education has taken root, the children themselves become their parents' teachers. Be that as it may, the village worker has to undertake adult education also.

Woman is described as man's better half. As long as she has not the same rights in law as man, as long as the birth of a girl does not receive the same welcome as that of a boy, so long we should know that India is suffering from partial paralysis. Suppression of woman is a denial of Ahimsa. Every village worker will, therefore, regard every woman as his mother, sister or daughter as the case may be, and look upon her with respect. Only such a worker will command the confidence of the village people.

It is impossible for an unhealthy people to win Swaraj. Therefore we should no longer be guilty of the neglect of the health of our people. Every village worker must have a knowledge of the general principles of health.

Without a common language no nation can come into being. Instead of worrying himself with the controversy about Hindi-Hindustani and Urdu, the village worker will acquire a knowledge of the Rashtrabhasha which should be such as can be understood by both Hindus and Muslims.

Our infatuation for English has made us unfaithful to provincial languages. If only as penance for this unfaithfulness the village worker should cultivate in the villagers a love of their own speech. He will have equal regard for all the other languages of India, and will learn the language of the part where he may be working, and thus be able to inspire the villagers there with a regard for their own speech.

The whole of this programme will, however, be a structure on sand if it is not built on the solid foundation of economic equality. Economic equality must never be supposed to mean possession of an equal amount of worldly goods by everyone. It does mean, however, that everyone will have a proper house to live in, sufficient and balanced food to eat, and sufficient Khadi with which to cover himself. It also means that the cruel inequality that obtains today will be removed by purely non-violent means.

THE VILLAGE AS THE NATION
MAKING OF THE INDIAN COMMON SENSE

Surinder S. Jodhka

The colonial writings on India were not simply a matter of mistaken assumptions or a set of 'fake news', as we understand the notion of misrepresentation in the present-day context. The colonial view evolved over a period of time. It had started to take shape even before the British administrators began to write on the nature of social life in the subcontinent. Its origin lay in the classical orientalist and Indological scholarship on the region. The Indologists and orientalists were a group of scholars spread across the countries of Europe who specialized in the study of classical languages, literatures, and traditions of the non-Western regions and cultures. India had been a source of fascination for Western scholars for a long time. However, their interest in India was not born merely out of a scholarly curiosity.

They began with the assumption that everything about India was different from their own society and culture, as it was unfolding during the nineteenth century. As Ronald Inden has very rightly pointed out, they saw the 'essence' of this difference, and of India, in the institution of caste which, in their view, was founded on a purely religious belief and was practised collectively.[1] It had no grounding in reason or individual choice, which were presumably features of Western cultures. Thus, unlike the West, where rationality was the founding norm, Indian culture was characterized by its opposite, where neither rationality nor politics played any role. According to this view, in the absence of individual agency and political conflict, the caste system and the social life of the Hindu in general had remained unchanged since ancient times. The colonial constructs of India in many ways extended and reinforced the self-aggrandizing view of the Western intellectual of the nineteenth century.

At another level, the emerging ideas of the Enlightenment and modernity also supported a binary view of the world. The world, as per this view, had evolved out of tradition into modernity; from myth to reason; from collective will to individual agency. Modernity, as sociologist Gurminder Bhambra argues, invoked the ideas of rupture and difference. Its advocates underlined that the societies of the modern West had gone through a process of a temporal rupture, a complete break from the agrarian ways of life in the past. The modernist conception of the world simultaneously also equated the agrarian societies of the non-Western world as being similar to the pasts of Western Europe. The difference between the West and the non-West was thus constructed in a manner that the two were viewed as being at different stages of their evolutionary process.[2]

The colonial formulations of India as being a land of village republics that had remained aloof from any kind of politics and outside influence, unchanged for centuries and millennia, were clearly born out of the emerging thinking in the West about non-Western societies and cultures. This paradigm for understanding the past, present, and future of human life also shaped social science theories of society, economy, and politics. They influenced the academia of the times and the emerging political elite, everywhere in the world. These formulations or constructs of the Indian society continue to be influential ways of thinking about social change even today. The Indian nationalist elite was no exception to this. Their views on the differences between 'rural' and 'urban' were clearly drawn from the colonial and modernist imaginations of India and the world. However, the Indian nationalists also turned these formulations around and made use of them in their own politics and political imaginations of the possible futures of India.

This chapter provides a brief glimpse into the writings of three of the most prominent political thinkers, who shaped the idea of India—Gandhi, Nehru, and Ambedkar—whose views on the village also reflect their visions for the 'free' nation. Their views of the Indian village were not mere political rhetoric invoked to counter the colonial power. They continued to shape state policy and political visions during the post-Independence period as well. In some senses, they are still invoked as sources of authority in popular deliberations on the nature of Indian tradition and its 'essential' qualities. The most influential of them has been Gandhi, whose ideas and ideological views on the 'village' are very widely known. However, as I show below, his views of the village evolved over time and underwent some important shifts.

Gandhi on Village and Village-ism

In a letter written to Jawaharlal Nehru in 1944, Gandhi had emphatically stated, 'For me, India begins and ends in the villages.'³ This was not the first time that he had made such a pronouncement. Nor was it the last. This had been a line he held for much of his political life. However, he was also not alone in making such an assertion. A large majority of the Indian nationalists, his contemporaries, such as Tagore, Nehru, and even Ambedkar, or those who came later, continued to make such claims. A closer reading of such a preoccupation with the village would also suggest that Gandhi, and others, did not deny the presence of cities or urban settlements, but saw them as being culturally alien to the native life of India. This is strange because this had never been the case. As we have discussed in the previous chapters, towns and cities had been a part of cultures and economies of the region for a very long time. As a matter of fact, Gandhi was himself born in a town, as were Nehru and Tagore. The coastal town of Porbandar, where Gandhi was born and where his ancestors had lived for many generations, was not a colonial city. It has a long history and finds reference even in popular Hindu mythology. Sudama, the poor Brahmin friend of Lord Krishna, is also believed to have hailed from the town of Porbandar.

However, Gandhi continued to underline the value of village in his writings all his life. His advocacy of such a view played an important role in converting the colonial idea of India as a land of villages into a common-sense and popular belief that pre-colonial India was indeed what the British had suggested. As is well known, he was the most ardent and persuasive advocate of the idea of 'the village being the soul of India'. However, his ideas and ideals evolved over time. Even though the village remained at the core of his vision of a free India, as well as in his social and political philosophy, his perception of it also underwent many changes as his engagement with the political process and the nationalist freedom struggle increased. An overview of his writings provides us a useful starting point for this chapter. This chapter will also provide a discussion of other contending views of the village that Gandhi's contemporaries articulated. Their views on the village also reflect their differing perspectives on the nature of India's past and visions for its future.

Early Preoccupations

Gandhi's preoccupation with the village begins with his growing involvement with public life. His invocation of the idea of the Indian village appears to have begun during his days in South Africa. There are at least three different stages in his engagement with the idea of the Indian village. In the first, he invoked it to distinguish Indians from the native black population of South Africa and thereby to establish an equivalence of the Indians living there with those from the 'civilized West', the whites.

In the second phase, he counterposed the social and cultural universe of the village against 'urban culture' in a binary construct. He identified urban with the colonizing spirit of the modernist West. In doing so, he proposed a critique of Western culture and civilization, which, in his view, had been a source of moral corruption for Indians. Thus, for him, true 'freedom' from British colonialism would require not just 'self-rule' but also a recovery of the 'lost self', the village.

The third phase of his engagement began with his visits to the actually existing villages of India, which proved to be a source of much disappointment. He thus, emphasized on the ways and means of reforming the village. However, this did not imply a shift away from the idea of the village. He continued to see it as an alternative way of living, a utopia, even when he found faults with the actual realities of rural life in the Indian countryside. As we know from historical writings on his evolution as a leader and a thinker, his views on possible alternatives to the western materialist modernity were also shaped by the writings of philosophers like Leo Tolstoy, H. D. Thoreau, and John Ruskin.[4] His views on village as a utopia, as he articulates them during this third phase, seem to also reflect those influences on him.

In the Racial Context of South Africa

It was perhaps in 1894 that Gandhi for the first time invoked the idea of the Indian village in quite a controversial political context. This was in a petition to the white government of South Africa, an 'open letter' written to the members of Legislative Assembly in Durban to demand voting rights for the people of Indian origin at par with the ruling English people. In a petition demanding racial separation of the Indians in South Africa from the native population of the blacks, he had argued that:

> In spite of the Premier's opinion to the contrary...I venture to point out that both the English and the Indians spring from a common stock, called the 'Indo-Aryan'.[5]

The idea of the village, as the British had framed it, was very important to his argument and he invoked it to further corroborate his point and establish equivalence between the Indians in South Africa and those belonging to the ruling white race. This is quite evident in his 'petition to the Natal Assembly', submitted in the same year, where he made reference to Sir Henry Maine's writings on the 'Indian village communities'. He argued that Maine had:

> ...most clearly pointed out that the Indian races have been familiar with representative institutions almost from the time immemorial.... The word panchayat is a household word throughout the length and breadth of India, and it means...a council of five elected by the class of the people whom the five belong, for the purpose of managing and controlling the social affairs of the particular caste.[6]

While demanding representation for Indians, Gandhi did not invoke any universal value of human equality. Nor did he refer to any of the popular thinkers of European Enlightenment and their ideas of freedom, fraternity, or equality. Instead, he invoked a kind of view that compared populations belonging to different 'racial stocks' and their differential levels of evolution. The Indians deserved the right to vote not because the idea of representation required universal franchise, but because of their being more evolved than the native black population, a certification of which was provided by a white man from Britain, and thus their eligibility for self-representation. By invoking the notion of the village panchayat and the five elected members as a representative institution, he also affirmed his approval of the hierarchical order of caste, which in his view, had been functioning as a representational channel in the Indian village for a long time.

The Village as 'Swaraj'

Gandhi's move from South Africa to India changed his political context and concerns. Though in some crucial sense his notion of the Indian village remained the same, his engagement with the idea of village became more critical and far more extensive. He also puts this idea to use very differently. An increasing involvement with the movement for independence had changed his political perspective towards the British colonizers. The question of securing voting rights for the Indian people and establishing equivalence with the whites was no longer his agenda. As he began assuming a leadership role in the struggle for independence, he saw himself in a greater oppositional role. The project was now to drive the colonial rulers out of India. The British had used the idea of India as a land of 'village republics' to legitimize their presence in the region. Waging a struggle for independence required the delegitimization of the British rule over India.

Gandhi did not give up on the 'village'. Instead, he turned the politics around it upside down. Gandhi built his narrative using the binary of village and city to produce an anti-colonial ideology. The village, he argued, represented the authentic self of India, its essence. It was simple and pure, self-reliant and self-governing. The modern cities, in contrast, were a colonial imposition. They symbolized domination and colonial plunder. His invocation of the village–city binary also extended to his vision of freedom or independence. Overthrowing of the colonial rule would bring self-rule, but only politically. Real self-rule or *swaraj* could only be achieved by restoring the civilizational strength of India, by a revival of its village communities. 'The uplift of India depended solely on the uplift of the villages'. The growth of big cities, particularly those established by the British, was no sign of progress. They were signs of degeneration, 'the real plague spots of India'.[7] Elsewhere, in a letter addressed to Lord Ampthill in 1909, he wrote:

> To me the rise of cities like Calcutta and Bombay is a matter for sorrow rather than congratulation. India has lost in having broken up a part of her village system.[8]

He elaborated it further in *Young India*, the newspaper he edited, in 1921:

> Our cities are not India. India lives in her seven and a half lakhs of villages, and the cities live upon the villages. They do not bring their wealth from other countries. The city people are brokers and commission agents for the big houses of Europe, America and Japan. The cities have cooperated with the latter in the bleeding process that has gone on for the past two hundred years.[9]

He reiterated this twenty-five years later, in 1946, speaking to industrial workers on how cities are exploitative settlements, and a part and parcel of the colonial rule:

> When the British first established themselves firmly in India their idea was to build cities where all rich people would gravitate and help them in exploiting the countryside. These cities were made partially beautiful; services of all kind were made available to

their inhabitants while the millions of villagers were left rotting in hopeless ignorance and misery.[10]

He underlined the village–city binary and its significance:

> The village civilisation and the city civilisation are totally different things. One depends on machinery and industrialisation, the other rests on handicrafts. We have given preference to the latter. After all, this industrialisation and large-scale production are only of comparatively recent growth. We do not know how far it has contributed to our development and happiness, but we know this much that it has brought in its wake the recent world wars....
>
> Our country was never so unhappy and miserable as it is at present. In the cities people may be getting big profits and good wages, but all that has become possible by sucking the blood of villagers.[11]

The city, for him, was also an immoral place from where rural folk picked up vices. Writing in another article he published in *Young India* in 1927, he pontificated:

> Some of the villages are deserted for six or eight months during the year. Villagers go to Bombay, work under unhealthy and often immoral conditions, then return to their villages during the rainy season bringing with them corruption, drunkenness and disease.[12]

Celebration of village life was perhaps also a strategic move for him, to shift the self-imagination of the nascent Indian nation away from the site of its birth, the urban middle class

119

and elite preoccupation, to the common people, the peasants and artisans living in the hinterlands. Ainslie Embree is perhaps right when he argues that such a move by Gandhi was also meant to give the masses of India 'a sense of involvement in the nation's destiny'. [13]

Until Gandhi arrived on the scene, the nationalist movement had largely been an urban phenomenon. 'For the early nationalist generations, independence meant being free to emulate colonial city life.'[14] By foregrounding the village as India, Gandhi managed to turn this view upside down. The nationalist leaders, who had nearly all been urban elite and who had acquired their political imagination either while studying in England or while working in the cities of Bombay, Calcutta, or Madras were no longer the sole torchbearers of the fight for independence. By arguing for the village as the site of 'India's soul', Gandhi was perhaps also asking for empathy for the poor masses and creating a space for them that was built on their legitimate claim and not simply born out of elite patronage.

As is evident from the discussion above, for Gandhi, the Indian village was not simply a place or a type of settlement; it also had a moral value, a design, a view of human life, which had the potential of providing an alternative to the technology-driven view of life of the Western city. He continued to invoke the text of the colonial scholar, Sir Henry Maine, while speaking for the village. Even as late as 1939, he wrote in *Harijan* that:

> ...Indian society was at one time unknowingly constituted on a non-violent basis. The home life, i.e.,

the village, was undisturbed by the periodical visitations from barbarous hordes. Maine has shown that India's villages were a congeries of republics.[15]

Reforming and Recovering the Self

Gandhi blamed the colonial rule and its policies for impairing the rural settlements, making them less creative and more dependent on the outside world. As he writes, 'the villager of today is not even half so intelligent or resourceful as the villager of fifty years ago.'[16] However, everything had not been lost. The spirit of the village could still be seen on ground, in the interior. He, for example, told a group of foreign visitors that if they truly wanted to 'see the heart of India', they ought to 'ignore big cities' as they were but poor editions of their big cities and

> Go thirty miles from the railway line, and you will see that the people show a kind of culture which you miss in the West...you will find culture which is unmistakable but far different from that of the West. Then you will take away something that may be worth taking.[17]

Gandhi's advocacy of the village was not to celebrate traditionalism; his was a plea for a kind of equality whereby the village is not treated as an inferior place. The village deserved a kind of autonomy, if India was to claim to be an independent nation:

> The cry of 'back to the village', some critics say, is putting back the hands of the clock of progress. But is it so? Is it going back to the village, or rendering back to

it what belongs to it? I am not asking the city-dwellers
to go to and live in the villages. But I am asking them
to render unto the villagers what is due to them.[18]

He found many flaws in the actually existing villages and did
not see all of their ills being a result of colonial rule or urban
influence. The two things that he vehemently campaigned
against, and saw as stemming from native culture, were the
practice of untouchability and a near absence of a general
sense of cleanliness. Compared to the cities, where people
were 'educated and broad-minded to a little extent at least',
untouchability was a more serious problem in the villages,
which were 'the centres of orthodoxy'. [19]

Not only did he ask the dominant communities of the
village to give up the practice of untouchability, he also called
upon those from the so-called untouchable castes to keep
themselves clean, 'refrain from eating meat of dead animals
and from drinking, send their children to schools, remove
untouchability among themselves and generally carry on
such reforms from within as is possible'.[20]

The problem of lack of hygiene was not confined to
the untouchable castes. He was often disappointed by the
disregard for cleanliness among the villagers in general:

> If we approach any village, the first thing we encounter
> is the dunghill and this is usually placed on raised
> ground. On entering the village, we find little difference
> between the approach and what is within the village.
> Here too there is dirt on the roads.... If a traveller who
> is unfamiliar with these parts comes across this state of
> affairs, he will not be able to differentiate between the

dunghill and the residential parts. As a matter of fact, there is not much of a difference between the two.[21]

In another piece, he praised the Europeans in Africa as being worthy of imitation:

There is no gainsaying the fact that our villager betrays a woeful ignorance of even the rudiments of village sanitation. One could deplore the race prejudice amongst the South African Europeans, but their attempts to keep their towns healthy and sanitary were heroic and worthy of imitation.[22]

Gandhi was keen on reviving aspects of traditional rural economy, particularly its 'defunct handicrafts', which could save the peasant from the ills of industrialization and the inevitability of moving to the cities.[23] However, he was also a reformist and asked for its 're-construction':

My idea of village swaraj is that it is completely republic, independent of its neighbours for its own vital wants, and yet interdependent for many others in which dependence is a necessity. Thus, every villager's first concern will be to grow its own food crops and cotton for its cloth.... Then if there is more land available, it will grow useful money crops, thus excluding ganja, tobacco, opium and the like.... Education will be compulsory up to the final basic course. As far as possible every activity will be conducted on the cooperative basis. There will be no castes such as we have today with their graded untouchability.... The government of the village will be conducted by a panchayat of five persons annually elected by the adult villagers, male and female, possessing minimum prescribed qualifications....[24]

For him, it was only in 'the simplicity of village' that a non-violent society could be imagined and realized. Given the size of India's population, Western-style urbanization would simply not be viable. 'Crores of people would never be able to live in peace with each other in towns'. However, 'simplicity' did not mean a complete disregard of modern science and modern means of communication. He also did not ask for a destruction of the existing urban centres. What he asked for was 'considerable revision' in their lifestyles, if the living standard of those living in the villages had to be improved.[25] Village, thus, becomes a utopia, an imaginary community, possessing all those qualities that are desirable for a nearly perfect living, collectively.

Though India's ruling elite have hardly taken his prescription seriously, Gandhi's ideas survive across a range of people. As the rural–urban inequalities grow, with the urban middle-class elite becoming increasingly hegemonic, and rural/agrarian India experiences further marginalization, Gandhi's views provide a useful intellectual resource for those who demand a more equitable growth.

His writings on the village offer a vision on the impending crises of ecology and environment and suggest alternative possibilities of development. India's growing urban mess, with increasing numbers of migrants arriving from rural areas as the sources of livelihood shrink in India's agrarian economy, make his suggestions all the more pertinent. However, his ideas have also been widely criticized. Many of his contemporaries, including those who worked with him, disagreed with him. The two most influential of these individuals are Jawaharlal Nehru and B. R. Ambedkar, whose views I present below.

Nehru the Modernist

Jawaharlal Nehru has perhaps been the most important and influential leader of India's nationalist movement after Gandhi. While he was one of Gandhi's loyal lieutenants until the latter's death in 1948 and agreed with him on most issues of national importance, Nehru's views and visions for the village, its past and future, significantly differed from those of Gandhi.

Most importantly perhaps, Nehru did not believe that in the 'village' lay the future of India, and he rarely ever identified himself with village life, or saw it as being morally superior to the city. This fact is important to emphasize because he was independent India's first prime minister. He was the catalyst of development planning and played a critical role in shaping its policies, including those of rural development and agrarian change. As with Gandhi, Nehru's writings too can be classified into distinct categories. Firstly, for him too, the idea of village is quite central to his notion of pre-colonial or traditional India, most of which draws from his readings of Western and colonial writings on the region. Secondly, his view of the Indian village also undergoes a change as he encounters 'the actually existing villages'. However, his prognosis of the ills caused by colonial rule differ significantly from those of Gandhi.

The Bourgeois Nehru

Nehru had little hesitation in admitting that until around 1920, his 'political outlook' had been that of his class, 'entirely bourgeois'.[26] It was only when he started his political career and came in direct contact with the common rural masses that he began to think differently. It was 'a new picture of India...naked, starving, crushed, and utterly miserable'.[27] Over the years he articulated his own understanding of history and specificities of Indian society and culture. They are perhaps best spelt out in his most famous book, *The Discovery of India* (first published in 1946).

Having been educated in Britain, he took the Eurocentric ideas of evolution and modernity as facts of life or modes of scientific thinking. The village was easily placed with other things that had presumably been features of traditional social arrangement in pre-modern societies everywhere. 'The autonomous village community, caste and the joint family', that he identified as the three basic concepts of the 'old Indian social structure', had something in common with traditional societies in general as the organizing principles were the same everywhere:

> In all these three it is the group that counts; the individual has a secondary place. There is nothing very unique about all this separately, and it is easy to find something equivalent to any of these three in other countries, especially in medieval times. [28]

He further elaborates his 'functionalist' and Eurocentric view of an integrated social order of the traditionalist village society:

...The functions of each group or caste were related to functions of the other castes, and the idea was that if each group functioned successfully within its own framework, then society as a whole worked harmoniously. Over and above this, a strong and fairly successful attempt was made to create a common national bond which would hold all these groups together—the sense of a common culture, common traditions, common heroes and saints, and common land to the four corners of which people went on pilgrimage. This national bond was of course very different from present-day nationalism; it was weak politically, but socially and culturally it was strong.[29]

Though Nehru did not celebrate the old 'village republics' of India as Gandhi did, the sources of their understanding of the pasts of the region were largely common—writings of colonial administrators and the Western scholars on India's past—and both accepted them uncritically.

Originally the agrarian system was based on a cooperative or collective village. Individuals and families had certain rights as well as certain obligations, both of which were determined and protected by customary law.[30]

He quotes, almost verbatim, what Metcalfe and later Marx said about the stability and autonomy of village life:

Foreign conquests brought war and destruction, revolts and their ruthless suppression, and new ruling classes relying chiefly on armed force.... The self-governing community, however, continued. Its break up began only under the British rule.[31]

He continues to argue that the traditional values emphasized 'the duties of the individual and the group' and not 'their rights'.

> The aim was social security: stability and continuance of the group; that is of society. Progress was not the aim, and progress therefore had to suffer. Within each group, whether it was the village community, the particular caste, or the large joint family, there was a communal life shared together, a sense of equality, and democratic methods.[32]

Quite like Gandhi, he believed that the idealized village had degenerated, with various ills becoming common practice; rigid hierarchies of caste was one of them.

> ...the ultimate weakness and failing of the caste system and the Indian social structure were that they degraded a mass of human beings and gave them no opportunities to get out of that condition—educationally, culturally, or economically.... In the context of society today, the caste system and much that goes with it are wholly incompatible, reactionary, restrictive, and barriers to progress. There can be no equality in status and opportunity within its framework, nor can there be political democracy, and much less, economic democracy.[33]

Beyond the Harmony of Caste and Community, the Kisans and Landlords

Unlike Gandhi, Nehru saw no virtues in reviving the traditional social structure, as the colonial and orientalist writings had presumably visualized or constructed it. The solution to the problem of caste, for him, lay in moving forward, towards a democratic and modern social order. As he travelled through the rural hinterlands, he was pained by the existing class disparities and the exploitative social order they produced. He often referred to the poverty and misery of peasants/kisans and the exploitative character of landlords. He described the landlords as a 'physically and intellectually degenerate' class, which had 'outlived their day'[34] and to 'the kisans, in the villages'[35] as constituting the real masses of India. Describing his first-hand experience of working with kisans, he writes:

> I listened to their innumerable tales of sorrow, their crushing and ever-growing burden of rent, illegal extraction, ejectments from land and mud hut, beatings; surrounded on all sides by vultures who preyed on them—zamindar's agents, moneylenders, police; toiling all day to find that what they produced was not theirs and their reward was kicks and curses and a hungry stomach.[36]

Landlordism had close ties with the colonial rule. The British rule had disturbed the old economic equilibrium of the village and implanted in its place the landlord system 'with disastrous results'.[37] It destroyed the local industry, the non-agricultural sources of employment:

The Indian farmer who used to supplement his income by plying the charkha in his spare time was also suddenly deprived of his extra income. Weavers, carders and dyers became unemployed. They were forced to fall back on the land for livelihood, by cultivating the land or by working as labourers, but there was already enough pressure on the land. The result was that the majority of the people were compelled to act as farm labourers, and somehow keep alive.... And this poverty began from the time the British came here because they started their own trade while destroying ours.[38]

He also felt dismayed at the politically docile and fatalistic nature of the Indian peasant, who, he believed:

...has an amazing capacity to bear famine, flood, disease, and continuous grinding poverty—and when he could endure it no longer; he would quietly and almost uncomplainingly lie down in his thousands or millions and die. That was his way of escape.[39]

Development Planning and India's Rural Futures

Nehru seemed to agree with Gandhi on the nature of traditional Indian village society and that the British colonial rule was responsible for disturbing its 'equilibrium'. However, his critique of the actually existing village lives was very different from that of Gandhi. He had no love for caste and found the 'class question' to be the primary issue that needed correction. While Gandhi spoke of the village as a community and advocated the need for its restoration, Nehru pointed to its irreconcilable class contradictions. While Gandhi desired a revival of the village community and a resolution of the class question through a spirit of trusteeship, Nehru advocated its social transformation through agrarian reforms and an economic change using modern technology.

The landlords were not to be 'trusted' but disenfranchized in free India. The kisans, the real 'masses of India', were being exploited and oppressed not only by the colonial state but also by the local landlords. Their difficulties 'in the main related to such questions as rent, ejectment and possession of lands'. 'Swaraj would be of little avail if it did not solve' the problems of the kisans, Nehru believed.[40] The Land Reforms introduced soon after Independence were a direct translation of such thinking. If agriculture was to develop, it was necessary that we put 'an end to *zamindari* and *jagirdari* systems. We must...eliminate all intermediaries and fix a limit for the size of holdings'.[41]

Nehru also disagreed with Gandhi on the value of modern industry and migrations of rural residents to cities. He had no desire to bring the presumed self-sufficient and autonomous village back. Industrial development and urbanization would be required for the building of a modern country, an integrated national economy. Addressing the Associated Chamber of Commerce in Calcutta in December 1947, he had said:

> ...while we want to help the peasants and agriculturalists, industry also is of dominant importance in India. Agriculture can produce wealth but it will produce more wealth (if) more people are drawn from agriculture and

put in industry. In fact, in order to improve agriculture, we must improve industry (sic). The two are allied.[42]

The only point of his agreement with Gandhi was the need for a revival of rural handicrafts and cottage industry. However, for Nehru, this was to be more for pragmatic economic reasons and not for a cultural revival of the traditional craft. He did not believe modern industry would be able to employ all the surplus rural population and an increasing use of technology was bound to release labour from agriculture. Thus, in India, the need was to encourage 'the village and cottage industry in a big way'.[43] Though 'the village could no longer be a self-contained economic unit...but it could very well be a governmental and electoral unit, each such unit functioning as a self-governing community within the larger political framework and looking after the essential needs of the village.... I feel sure that the village should be treated as a unit. This will give truer and more responsible representation.'[44]

Thus, despite their differences on the possible futures of India's village, Nehru was not untouched by the influence of Gandhi. Or, perhaps, he was trying to accommodate the Gandhian world view by bringing it into the policy domain. As we have seen in the discussion above, despite his modernist outlook to nation building, Nehru did carry a positive view of the pre-colonial village community as had been presented by the colonial and orientalist writers. It was left to B. R. Ambedkar to develop a critique of the idea of the 'village community', invoking his own personal experiences of caste hierarchy as an 'untouchable' himself.

Ambedkar, the 'Anti-village' Advocate

Gandhi and Nehru were the most prominent leaders of India's freedom movement. They also shaped the popular imaginations of the emerging nation, of its pasts and its possible futures. Though the core of their audience was the emerging urban middle class, their influence went far beyond. They emerged as the icons for a cross-section of Indian society and the post-Independence state system of India. While Nehru became the prime minister of the country and remained in the chair until his death, Gandhi too occupied an important symbolic space in the life of the new nation. His picture continues to appear on Indian currency notes. Their views of the village have also been critical in shaping policies and programmes of development and representation.

Perhaps the third most important leader who played a critical role in the making of modern India is B. R. Ambedkar. Though he was not a part of the Indian National Congress, he took up the task of drafting the Indian Constitution, helping the Constituent Assembly put together its proposals and also influencing it through his knowledge of law, as it had come to be practised in the democratic countries of the West. He was perhaps the most educated member of the Constituent Assembly, with two doctorates from two of the most prominent institutions of higher learning in the modern Western world—Columbia University and the London School of Economics. He was thus trained not only to practise law at the bar but also equipped with the skills of a social science researcher.

His vision of India, the social composition of its settlements (villages, towns, and cities), and possible pathways to take it forward on the road to becoming a modern democratic society were also shaped by his own experience, as a scholar and as a 'victim' of the prevailing order of caste. Over the years after his death, he has consistently grown in stature. As Eleanor Zelliot points out, he is perhaps the only pre-Independence leader who has continued to grow in fame and influence throughout the contemporary period.[45]

Village as the Den of Untouchability

Despite his exceptional educational accomplishments, Ambedkar was not allowed to forget his social background, his belonging to an untouchable caste. And despite his equally monumental contribution to the making of the Indian Constitution, he remains a leader with a specific caste identity, popularly viewed as a champion of Dalit rights. He indeed fought for their rights all his life, but his writings also provide a sociological perspective on the Indian society: on village life, caste, gender, law, and many other subjects.

Much like Gandhi and Nehru, Ambedkar too was born in an urban setting, in the cantonment town of Mhow in present-day Madhya Pradesh. His family too had been urban and hailed from Ambadawe, a town in the Ratnagiri district of Maharashtra. His father was employed with the colonial army and had earned the rank of subedar. However, despite having all the credentials that set him outside the rural order of caste, he had to frequently experience humiliation owing to his caste identity. These experiences significantly influenced his understanding of village life. The village, for him, was 'the working plant of the Hindu social order' where one could observe 'the Hindu social order in operation in full swing'.[46] Far from being a harmonious community, the village for him was a divided universe and caste was its basis:

> The Hindu society insists on segregation of the untouchables. The Hindu will not live in the quarters of the untouchables and will not allow the untouchables to live inside Hindu quarters.... It is not a case of social separation, a mere stoppage of social intercourse for a temporary period. It is a case of territorial segregation and of a cordon sanitaire putting the impure people inside the barbed wire into a sort of a cage. Every Hindu village has a ghetto. The Hindus live in the village and the untouchables live in the ghetto.[47]

The divisions that marked a typical village were not hard to see: it was divided into two sets of populations: the 'touchable' groups and the 'untouchable' groups. The touchables formed, what he called, 'the major community' and the untouchables 'a minor community'. The former lived inside the village and the latter were made to live outside the village in separate quarters.

> The touchables were economically the dominant community and commanded power; the untouchables were a 'dependent community' and a 'subject race of hereditary bondsmen'. The untouchables lived according to the codes laid down for them by the dominant 'touchable' major community. These codes laid guidelines regarding their habitations; the distance

they ought to maintain from the 'Hindus'; the dress they should wear; the houses they should live in; the language they should speak; the names they should keep. They could not build houses having tiled roofs; they could not wear silver or gold jewellery.[48]

Like Gandhi and Nehru, Ambedkar too wrote extensively on different aspects of Indian society and the colonial rule. The social structure of the village and caste appear very frequently in his writings. However, some of his arguments were best crystallized during the debates in the Constituent Assembly where some 'Hindu members' had passionately argued in favour of making the village an autonomous administrative unit with its own legislature, executive, and judiciary. Ambedkar had vehemently opposed such a move:

I hold that these village republics have been the ruination of India.... What is the village but a sink of localism, a den of ignorance, narrow-mindedness and communalism?[49]

Such a recognition of the village as a unit of the legal structure of India would have been 'a great calamity' for those who lived on its periphery, the untouchables, he argued.[50]

While Gandhi and Nehru had accepted the colonial construct of 'village community' as a reality of India's past, Ambedkar looked at it more critically. Given his training in the social sciences, he was able to locate the source of this construct in the orientalist narratives of India. He also provided a sociological explanation for its uncritical acceptance by the middle-class elite of India. 'The average

Hindu was always in ecstasy whenever he spoke of the Indian village. He regarded it as an ideal form of social organisation to which he believed there was no parallel anywhere in the world.'[51]

However, the 'realistic picture' of village life was very different. The so-called village community was nowhere close to being democratic. Life in the village was marked by cultures of exclusion, denials, and discrimination. 'When the whole village community was engaged in celebrating a general festivity such as Holi or Dasara, the untouchables must perform all menial acts which were preliminary to the main observance. These duties had to be performed without remuneration.'[52]

The Republic of Untouchability

Ambedkar underlined that besides their complete domination, the untouchables were also exploited and oppressed by the upper castes. They were not allowed to acquire wealth in the form of land or cattle; they could not practise agriculture. Even as labourers they could not demand reasonable wages and had to submit to the rates fixed or suffer violence.[53] They lived a life that was full of humiliation and dependency. There was only one source of livelihood open to them. It was 'the right to beg food from the Hindu farmers of the village. A large majority of the untouchables in the village were either servants or landless labourers. As village servants, they depended on the Hindus for their maintenance, and had to go from door to door every day and collect bread or cooked food from the Hindus in return for certain customary services rendered by them to the Hindus.'[54]

This is the village republic of which the Hindus are so proud. What is the position of the untouchables in this Republic? They are not merely the last but are also the least.... (I)n this Republic there is no place for democracy. There is no room for equality. There is no room for liberty and there is no room for fraternity. The Indian village is a very negation of Republic. The Republic is an Empire of the Hindus over the untouchables. It is a kind of colonialism of the Hindus designed to exploit the untouchables. The untouchables have no rights.... They have no rights because they are outside the village republic and because they are outside the so-called village republic, they are outside the Hindu fold.[55]

Ambedkar extended his view of the village to his perspective on Indian society. Beginning with the village, he asserted that this culture of caste domination prevailed all over. 'From the capital of India down to the village level the whole administration is rigged by the Hindus. The Hindus are like the omnipotent almighty pervading all over the administration in all its branches having its authority in all its nooks and corners.'[56]

Ambedkar also rejected the popular anthropological theories of caste that highlighted the ideological unity of the Hindu society and claimed that the untouchables too subscribed to ideas of purity and pollution. There was no such cultural consensus or a willing acceptance of the hierarchical order.

The four varnas were animated by nothing but a spirit of animosity towards one another. There would not be slightest exaggeration to say that the social history of the Hindus is not merely of class struggle but class war fought with such bitterness that even the Marxists will find it difficult to cite parallel cases to match.... It seems that the first class-struggle took place between the Brahmins, Kshatriyas and Vaishyas on the one hand and the Shudras on the other.[57]

Ambedkar, thus, had no great appreciation for the village. The ground realities of the actually existing villages were well understood by him and became a source of his critique of the undemocratic spirit of Indian society. The village, for him, was a 'model' of the Hindu society, a microcosm of the Hindu social order, marked by hierarchies of caste and a culture of exclusion and discrimination, best reflected in caste-based spatial divisions within the rural settlements.

Making of the National Common Sense

Thus, despite their different trajectories, Gandhi, Nehru and Ambedkar all began with the same construct of the Indian village. Each saw the Indian village essentially as a Hindu village, composed of caste groupings and marked by differences and inequalities. While Nehru foregrounded the realities of class, Ambedkar pointed to the divisions of caste. Gandhi recognized the presence of both caste as well as class. And while he acknowledged that these differences and inequalities were undesirable, he firmly believed that the collective spirit of the traditional community had the potential of overcoming them. He did not principally oppose the idea of caste-based divisions, but considered the practice of untouchability as unacceptable, and needing reform.

Similarly, class divisions within the village could be overcome through trusteeship. Both Gandhi and Nehru were in favour of preserving the village, albeit in a reformed version. Nehru was keen on modernizing its agriculture through technology and a redistribution of land, while Gandhi believed in a completely different paradigm of life, which was not driven by a desire for endless consumption. Village life, for him, was also a morally superior way of living, in which lay an alternative to capitalist modernity.

Ambedkar differed with both of them on a fundamental level. He had no sympathy for village life. Unlike Gandhi and Nehru, he did not accept the colonial view of the village community as a historical account of India's past. For him, it was an orientalist construct. The actually existing village had no community spirit. On the contrary, it was a site of caste-based oppression, exclusion, and exploitation.

Not only was there no place for Dalits to live in the village with dignity, the so-called spirit of village community was also antithetical to democracy. The Indian villages, thus, needed a radical transformation. For his fellow Dalits, his prescription was to abandon the village, and to move to towns and cities. Not that caste was absent there, but it was perhaps easier to escape it in the city than it was in the village.

Together, the writings and reflections of Gandhi, Nehru, and Ambedkar also became a source of popular common sense about the nature of Indian society and its pasts. Notwithstanding their differences, there are many ways in which the three seem to agree. They all spoke about the village in civilizational terms. The Indian village had a pan-Indian character, with no regional variations, of caste, community, or ecology. Villages of Punjab or Bengal were viewed as similar to those of Kerala or Kashmir. They also showed no awareness of the significant regional differences in the nature of caste hierarchies, or their dynamics across different religious and regional communities. They, thus, accepted the orientalist and colonial view that the village was the core of India and that it was the social universe of the Hindus. None of them made any reference to a Muslim or Sikh or tribal village in colonial India. By giving such credence to the orientalist view of India's past, they not only shaped the popular imaginations of the emerging urban middle classes but also of the social sciences.

Nevertheless, it should be remembered that though orientalist/colonial categories such as 'village' provided them with conceptual resources, these categories did not completely limit/determine their politics and world views. Their substantive notions of empirical reality were shaped by a multitude of factors, and the effects of their uses of such categories varied significantly. They were all unhappy with the existing state of affairs in the Indian village but had different prescriptions about the nature and modes of change required. Their ideas and visions for rural futures also shaped independent India's policies for social change and rural development.

THE RAT'S GUIDE

Amitava Kumar

Rats have burrowed under the railway tracks in Patna. As citizens of a literal underworld, I imagine the rats inhabiting a spreading web of small safe houses and getaway streets. We could choose to call it a city under the city, or if that is too sophisticated a description for at least one of the two entities, then let's just call it a dense warren of subterranean burrows. In places, the railway platform has collapsed. In my mind's eye, I watch a train approaching Patna Junction in the early morning. The traveller sees the men sitting beside the tracks with their bottoms exposed, plastic bottles of water on the ground in front of them, often a mobile phone pressed to the ear. But at night the first inhabitants of Patna that the visitor passes are the invisible ones: warm, humble, highly sociable, clever, fiercely diligent rats.

In the library at Patna University, I heard that rats had taken over a section of the stacks and the library was closed. Also, there are rats—always in these stories, rats as big as cats—in the Beur Jail. After he was shifted there from an air-conditioned clubhouse that had served as a makeshift prison, the jail was home for a while to the former chief minister, Lalu Prasad Yadav. He tended a vegetable garden in prison and issued orders to visiting politicians and bureaucrats. Another inmate of Beur Jail is the former parliamentarian, Pappu Yadav, on trial for the murder of a communist leader, but awarded degrees in human rights and disaster management while behind bars. But, I digress.

For some reason, even in the Patna Museum, home to Mauryan art and Buddhist relics, including, some say, the ashes of Lord Buddha, there are stuffed rats nailed to black wooden bases. About fifty feet away stands the magnificent, glistening third century BCE sculpture of the Didarganj Yakshi. A long and heavy necklace dangles in the gap between her globular stone breasts. In her right hand, she holds a fly-whisk flung languidly over her shoulder. And running away from her are the stuffed rats, a small procession of them, rotting and seemingly blinded with age, breathing the air of eternity under dusty glass.

Outside in the city, however, and, one can be certain, in other parts of the museum too, the rats are alive and dangerous. Newspapers periodically carry reports that babies have been bitten by rats. One such report helpfully explained that it was the traces of food on the unwashed faces of infants that attracted the rodents. Rats are curious, especially about food, and they will eat anything. In the hospital in Patna where my sister works, nurses play the radio at night because they are firmly of the belief that the music keeps the rats from nibbling at their toes.

In the middle of the night one winter, during a visit to Patna, I was sitting at the dining table with my jet-lagged two-year-old, watching a cartoon on my computer. I had only switched on a single, dim light as I didn't want my parents to be disturbed. We must have been sitting there quietly for about half an hour before my little boy asked, 'Baba, what is that?' He was pointing beyond the screen.

There were two enormous rats walking away from us. They looked like stout ladies, on tiny heels, on their way to the market. I wouldn't have been surprised to see them carrying small, elegant handbags.

The next morning, when my son told my wife about the rats he had seen—he was confused at first and said they were rabbits—my wife was alarmed. But no one else was. Despite how ubiquitous the rats were in Patna, or perhaps *because* they were ubiquitous, no one seemed to pay much attention. I would bring them up in conversation, and people would laugh and launch into stories. One person told me that the Patna police had claimed that rats were drinking from the bottles of illegal liquor seized by the authorities and stored in warehouses. I didn't believe the story—I said that I smelled a rat—and so a link was duly sent to me. In the press report, a senior police officer named Kundan Krishnan was quoted as saying, 'We are fed up with these drunken rats and cannot explain why they have suddenly turned to consumption of alcohol.'

For a while I had hoped to get a professional pest control agency to come and trap rats in the house in Patna. The problem was a pressing one—rats had carried away my mother's dentures. But all I could find was a man who would come and put packets of 'rat poison' in different rooms. People suggested that I buy traps and put food inside; the same people admitted that the rats were too smart to get caught in such traps. I detected a note of pride in such statements. My sister told me that her hospital had bought an expensive piece of ultrasonic machinery which emitted a high-frequency sound that kept rats away. The sound was inaudible to human ears, and my sister said that things were okay for a while. Then, they noticed that a rat had bitten through the electric cord and, since then, the machine had simply stood unused in a corner.

We were visiting Patna from upstate New York. Just a month earlier, *New York* magazine had run a feature on rats, calling them 'one of evolution's more triumphant guilty pleasures'.[1] Rats are one of New York City's obsessions. They are neither as invincible as bed bugs, nor as common as cockroaches, but they make for more scary YouTube videos. Of course, no trip to the waterfront goes unrewarded by a rat-sighting, and they are a constant feature of the city's subways and sewers. During those nights in Patna, when I lay awake in bed listening to the movement of rats in the dark, odd details from the *New York* magazine article would come to me. Rats can get pregnant within eighteen hours of having given birth, and can produce a litter twenty-one days after impregnation. They can swim for more than half a mile, tread water for three days, and, as my mother also alleged, sometimes even emerge through the toilet bowl. They can gnaw through concrete and collapse their skeletons to fit through a hole no bigger than a coin. Rats can also go two weeks without sleeping.

I didn't find an exterminator in Patna. In his place, I met a man who wanted rats to be killed for food. Vijoy Prakash is a senior official in the Bihar administration: principal secretary in the Department of Rural Development; and he has caused controversy by suggesting that restaurants should have rat meat on their menu. Questions about this proposal were raised in the Bihar Legislature, and the papers had reported it with some relish. I met Prakash in his office in the Old Secretariat in Patna. He was a kind-looking man, quiet and dark-skinned, his eyebrows flecked with grey. In the spacious, air-conditioned office, Prakash was working on a report on his desk. I looked around while I waited. A wooden board to my right had the names of administrators who had served in that office. The names were carefully painted in white on the varnished wood. Number 22 on that list, the last name, was Prakash's. I noted with pleasure, and surprise, that Number 7 on that list was my father. My father, who retired from service long ago, must have occupied the chair on which Prakash was now sitting, when I was still a student. Did I ever visit my father in this room, bringing him lunch during a trip home? I couldn't remember if I did.

Prakash, who trained as an astrophysicist, is a rationalist. He wants people to have more enlightened views about nature and society. His mission, I realized when we began talking, isn't simply to change the popular perception of rats. Instead, it is to alter the views that most people have of a particular community near the bottom of the social ladder: the Musahars, known all over Bihar as the rat-eating caste. Prakash says that rats trapped in fields have long been a part of the Musahars' diet and there is no reason why others cannot also benefit from protein-rich rat meat. His main point was to engineer change in the living conditions of the Musahars who are among the poorest and most marginalized groups in Bihar. If rats were accepted as a popular food item, and as a consequence rat-farming was commercialized, the Musahars would see an automatic rise in their income. Like every good bureaucrat I've met, Prakash rattled off statistics to support his theory. In 1961, the rate of literacy among Musahars was merely 2.5 per cent; forty years later, the rate of literacy had risen to only 9 per cent. So far as rats were concerned, in a country and state where a significant percentage of people went hungry, rats ate 30 to 40 per cent of the crops. In each rat hole excavated in a field, you could find up to thirteen to fourteen kilograms of grain. When these two facts are appraised side-by-side, Prakash pointed out, his plan made even more sense.

I wasn't entirely convinced, but Prakash was unfazed by my scepticism. He said that even as recently as fifty years ago, chicken wasn't allowed in many homes in Patna. It was just a matter of time before rats would be 'domesticated' and eaten in homes.

'Have you eaten a rat?' I asked.

'Yes,' he said. In the Musahar toli in Naubatpur. He had gone there with his wife, a teacher, and they had been invited to have lunch with the family they were visiting. The rats had been fried and then cooked in a curry. The dish was served with rice and tasted delicious. I had known Musahar families in my village in Champaran. In fact, once when I was a boy, I had just finished bathing at the handpump a little distance from my grandmother's house when a woman approached me. Behind her was a child wearing a ragged pair of shorts. He was younger than me, maybe seven or eight years old. I remember very clearly that the woman was tall, she had curly hair, and her sari was mustard-coloured. She asked me politely when I was going to return to Patna. My father had said we were to leave in an hour.

'Can't you take him with you?'

I had seen the woman before in the village. I don't think I had spoken to her. The boy was trying to hide behind his mother. The woman spoke again because I had said nothing.

'He will play with you. He will do all the work that needs to be done in the house. Take him with you. There is not enough here for him to eat.'

I went back to the house and pointed out the woman to my mother or an aunt. Somebody recognized her. I was told that she was a Musahar. She wanted her son to be a servant in our home in Patna. We were upper-caste and I was told that my grandmother would not allow a Musahar to step inside the house.

ᔕ

Many years would pass before I would read Phanishwar Nath Renu's memoir about doing relief work during the flood caused by the waters of the Mahananda in 1949.[2] Kerosene was needed, and matches, and medicine for feet that were rotting from prolonged exposure to water. Renu, along with a doctor, travelled through the flood-hit areas in a boat. He wrote that they had heard that for several days the Musahars had been eating any fish and rats that they managed to singe over a fire. Once the two of them reached the flooded basti they heard the sound of the dhol and cymbals. A platform had been erected over the water and served as a stage. A dance was in progress. Wearing a red sari, a dark-skinned Musahar man was pretending to be a bride; behind the figure in the sari was the husband, begging her to come back home. But the bride refused, complaining about her abusive mother-in-law and her sister-in-law's sharp tongue. It was now the husband's turn to sing a song. He promised to break his sister's legs, and to push his mother out of the house. The audience, smeared with mud, and hungry, was full of laughter. In the course of writing this book, like the great writer Renu, I would sometimes find joy amongst those I had expected only to be burdened by pathos. Joy is less common, no doubt, but is as real as suffering. Writers often marshal inordinate zeal when portraying the misery of the downtrodden and the oppressed: it is only a form of narcissism; the writer enamoured of his or her sensitive self faithfully recording the pain of others. No doubt I am guilty of this too, but I plead equal fondness for folly, pleasure, guile, greed, and hypocrisy. Hence, the rats.

The day after I met Vijoy Prakash in his office in Patna I went with my father to our village. The journey used to take several hours but I was told that it now took half the time to reach our destination because of a new bypass that had been built in order to promote tourism to nearby Buddhist sites like the stupa near Kesaria. (This is a Bihar specialty. No one tells you the distance between two places in kilometres; instead, because everything depends on the condition of the roads, distance is always discussed in terms of time.) Of course, there were delays. A long line of trucks idled on the side of the road. The highway had been blocked by angry youth demonstrating because of the death of a man injured in an accident. The victim had been taken to a nearby government hospital, but as no doctor had shown up for work for several days; the man succumbed to his injuries. The protestors had made a truck driver park his vehicle across the road, and, for good measure, also put a log and broken furniture in the path of approaching vehicles. We had no option but to turn back. For a while, even this was not allowed. I first showed sympathy to the gathered youth but then took out my press pass and threatened them with severe consequences if we were not allowed on our way. They relented after a while, and we took narrow rural roads around the blockage, and re-emerged on to the highway after about half an hour.

I was returning to my ancestral home for the first time since my grandmother's death more than a decade ago. On the small platform with the tulsi plant, where my grandmother had poured water each morning, someone had laid a fresh hibiscus. But other than that small touch, a look of decay pervaded the house. I walked through the empty corridors and looked at the locked doors of the uninhabited rooms where I had spent all my holidays. A feeling of great melancholy washed over me. Suddenly, alone in an empty corridor, I began to weep. I missed my grandmother's voice, or maybe only my childhood. In any case, I didn't linger. I had come here on a small anthropological mission, not to surrender to nostalgia. I wanted a Musahar to show me how he caught a rat.

Sinhasan, a mild-mannered, middle-aged man I remembered from the past, was working on the construction of a hospital near our ancestral house that our family was funding. It would be named after my grandmother. My father had made the journey to check how work on the project was going. Sinhasan, a Musahar, didn't want to put me to any trouble. He said I could sit in the shade; he would go into the fields, catch the rats, and bring them to me.

'No,' I said, 'you don't understand. I want to observe how you catch them.'

He called out to two other men, also Musahars, and we started walking to the fields. One of the men was carrying a kudaal for digging. The monsoon rains had left the ground soft and wet. My shoes sank in the mud. Sinhasan said that it was very easy to catch rats before the rains, early in the summer, when the wheat had ripened and was still standing in the fields.

'Rats make holes and save a lot of grain for their young. They are hopping around at that time, and we catch them and cook them right here.'

'How do they taste?' I asked.

'Good,' he said.

'Is it like chicken?' Sinhasan paused for a second and then said, 'Murgi se zyaada taiyaar hai.' It is better than chicken.

At the edge of a field, where it was drier, the men stopped. They had seen a little mound of freshly-dug earth. The man with the kudaal was named Phuldeo. He showed me a few scattered grains lying underfoot, evidence of a rat nearby, and then he began to dig. The day was so hot and humid that within a minute or two sweat was dripping off Phuldeo's nose and chin. The little trench he was digging was about two feet wide and by the time he finished, it was four feet in length. I saw that Sinhasan and the third man, whose name was Chapraasi, had positioned themselves on either side of the trench. Both men were around forty, with thin, sinewy limbs. They looked sturdy but had both adopted such a relaxed stance that I got a bit worried. When I asked if the rat wouldn't get away, Sinhasan smiled and brushed aside my question.

Phuldeo said he could see the rat hole. Two more heaves, and he bent down. The rat's snout was visible to him. A quick flick of his hand and he had caught it. Phuldeo held it up, and I saw its lower incisors, which were long and curved. They were a dirty yellow, the colour of old toenails. Sinhasan said, 'If it doesn't cut with those teeth night and day, those teeth will go right through its head. It can eat through brick. Even when it's sleeping, its mouth keeps moving.'

I said that I wanted to take a picture and in that moment, while Phuldeo tried to give me a better view of the rat's head, it bit him on the finger. Blood spurted out. I took pictures of the tiny ears, the luxuriant hairs around its nose, and above those dirty yellow teeth, the glinting black eyes.

We let the rat return to the field. My Musahar informants told me that in the right season they ate rats about three or four times a week. Four or five of them were enough for a meal. How did they cook the meat? Over a small fire, the hair was first burned off the body; a small incision was then made in the belly to remove the entrails; following this, spices were rubbed into the meat, and it was fried. I had one last question to put to Sinhasan. A senior bureaucrat in Patna had said to me that people were judged by what they ate. The reason Musahars were looked down upon in Bihar was that they ate rats. The official believed that if we all began to think about rats in a more positive way, caste itself would disappear and we would no longer think of Musahars as a lower caste. Did this make sense to them? Did they share the official's optimism?

Sinhasan didn't have to consider this question too long. He said, 'Only if everyone else is already of the same view as the official. Then, yes, people's sense of caste will change. Otherwise, no.'

Sinhasan was being polite. He was taking care not to throw the question back in my face. High-minded abstractions weren't among his pressing concerns. His worry was finding food for that day and the next. In another five minutes he was going to return to work, mixing cement to build the front brick wall of the hospital. For the day's labour he was going to be paid ₹150. A generation ago there would have been work only in the landlord's fields, and now there were other kinds, mostly in small industries, and payment in cash. But the conditions of work, and even its availability, were dismal. For those at the bottom of the social ladder, there was only harsh physical labour. The two other men, balanced on bamboo beams behind Sinhasan, flinging water on the bricks and then cementing them, were also Dalits. In the distance, on the patio of my old ancestral home, upper-caste men were sitting on cots. They were poor too, eking out a living as farmers, but none of them was ever likely do Sinhasan's work. One of them, wearing a lungi, his bare feet cracked, had followed me out to where I was talking to Sinhasan. This man told me that he had eaten roasted rats when he was a boy playing in the fields. Age had brought him an awareness of his social status and he had stopped going near rats. He knew the consequences of breaking taboos. 'Sikaayat ho jaayi.' People would complain.

We drove back to Patna. Once again, there was a delay. Traffic was stalled on the highway: a speeding bus had knocked down a motorcyclist. A red motorcycle lay crushed under its wheel. A part of the tarmac was wet. Was it blood—

or oil from the bike? I didn't get out of the car to find out. A fire had been lit in the middle of the road. Once again, I needed to show my press pass.

We were on the highway to progress. It was littered with fresh carnage. This cliché appeared in my mind even before we had left the scene of the accident. Change was visible everywhere. Even our village had changed. The small stores where I once used to buy small packets of Parle-G biscuits were now selling mobile phones. The real changes were less visible. Nearly twenty women in the village earned government pay, working on child development schemes. Political and financial power was no longer limited to the upper caste. A few backward-caste families had prospered: my grandfather had once been mukhiya but sometime in my teens, the village elected a new headman, a man from a lower caste. In the last election, because of the implementation of reservation policy, the village barber was elected mukhiya. This was an improvement, even if the ideological gains exceeded material ones and left far too many people behind. The most impoverished group, the Dalits, had improved their lot, but not by very much. Over the last decade, the Musahars of my childhood had made their way out of bondage to land; men like Phuldeo also worked as labourers in Punjab and Andhra, they rode on trucks to other parts of the country, but they owned next to nothing. At the same time, the world outside had changed. The village appeared only a stone's throw away from the world of television broadcasting stations and even beauty parlours. A pukka road, shaded by newly planted trees, now connected the village to the nearby town. The villagers didn't even need to make a journey to

Patna, which had been the main city when I was young; now they boarded trains that took them directly to Mumbai and Hyderabad. The Bihar of my childhood was now gone, replaced by something entirely new.

'OH, THAT HOUSE? IT'S IN THE
SEA NOW—THERE!'

Rahul M.

Google Maps tells me I am approaching my destination. But the neighbourhood appears a bit altered from what I remember of it. There's no sign of the crumbling old house by the sea, whose coordinates I had saved on my phone the last time I visited Uppada. 'Oh, that house? It is in the sea now—there!' says T. Maramma, casually pointing to a wave gushing in from the Bay of Bengal.

I vividly remember the old structure that had offered a stunning, yet sombre, backdrop as I photographed Maramma and her family members a few weeks before the nationwide lockdown of March 2020. Perched perilously on a narrow beach, it was the only portion remaining of what used to be a large home where Maramma's joint family lived until the early years of this century.

'It was a building with eight rooms and three sheds [for animals]. Around a hundred people used to live here,' says Maramma, a small-time local politician in her fifties, who once ran a fish business. A cyclone that hit Uppada just before the 2004 tsunami took away a big chunk of the building, forcing the joint family to move into different houses. Maramma continued to use the old structure for a few more years before shifting to a house nearby.

Maramma and her family are not alone; nearly everyone in Uppada seems to have moved home at least once because of the encroaching sea. Their calculations on when to quit a house are based on lived experience and the local community's instinctive reading of the seas. 'We can sense that the house will go into the sea when the waves start to bulge forward. Then we move our utensils and everything to one side [and start searching for a temporary house to rent]. The old house usually goes [into the sea] within a month,' explains O. Siva. At fourteen, he has already had to leave one house to escape the sea.

٭

Located in East Godavari district, along the 975-kilometre coastline of Andhra Pradesh, Uppada has witnessed a steady onslaught by the sea for as long as its residents can remember.

When Maramma's family moved into their then new home around fifty years ago, it was located far from the beach. 'Our legs used to ache a lot when we walked home from the shore,' recalls O. Chinnabbai, Siva's grandfather and Maramma's uncle. A deep-sea fisherman in his seventies or eighties, he remembers a time when the stretch leading from their home to the beach was dotted with houses, shops, and a few government buildings. 'That was where the shore was,' Chinnabbai points towards a distant horizon where some ships fade into the evening sky.

'Between our new house and the sea, there was a lot of sand too,' Maramma reminisces. 'When we were children, we would play in the sand mounds and slide through them.'

Much of the Uppada of these memories now lies submerged in the sea. Between 1989 and 2018, Uppada's coastline eroded, on average, 1.23 metres every year; in 2017–18, the erosion was as much as 26.3 metres, says a study by researchers at the Andhra Pradesh Space Applications Centre, Vijayawada. Another study noted that over the last four decades the sea has claimed more than 600 acres of land in the Kakinada suburbs—with Uppada, in Kakinada division's Kothapalle mandal, alone losing around one-fourth of that. A 2014 study quoted fisherfolk living along the coast north of Kakinada as saying that the beach had shrunk by several hundred metres over the last twenty-five years.

'The coastal erosion at Uppada, a few kilometres north of Kakinada town, is caused mainly by the growth of Hope Island—scientifically known as a 'spit'—a 21-kilometre-long linear sand body. That spit grew naturally northward from the mouth of Nilarevu, a distributary of Godavari River,' says Dr Kakani Nageswara Rao, a retired professor of the department of geo-engineering, Andhra University, Visakhapatnam. 'The waves refracted by the spit are impinging on the Uppada coast, leading to its erosion. Probably initiated more than a century ago, this sand spit more or less attained its present form in the 1950s,' explains the professor, who has been closely studying the coastal forms and processes along the Andhra coast for several decades.

Official records dating back to the early 1900s confirm that the Uppada phenomenon was already recognized more than a century ago. The *Godavari District Gazetteer* of 1907, for example, notes that the sea had eroded more than 50 yards of land at Uppada since 1900—in other words, the village lost seven metres of land every year in those seven years.

'Since coastal zones in general are very dynamic regions, with the interplay of complex global, regional, and local phenomena,' says Dr Rao, 'the reasons for coastal erosion at Uppada are multidimensional.' Global warming, melting polar ice caps and rising sea levels, besides increased frequency of cyclones in the Bay of Bengal, are a few of them. A drastic reduction in sediment loads at the river mouths, caused by burgeoning dams in the Godavari basin, further exacerbates the situation.

✎

As its land disappears into the sea bit by bit, Uppada gets recreated in the memory of its people.

One of the villagers asks me to watch the Telugu movie *Naakuu Swatantram Vachindi* for a glimpse of the village that resides in their memories and their stories. I see a different Uppada in the 1975 film: the village and the sea lie at a comfortable distance from each other, a gorgeous sandy beach separating them. The sea and sand, captured in single-frame shots—the beach was wide enough to allow the crew to shoot from various angles—form the background to key sequences in the film.

'I watched the shooting of the film. Some of the actors who came for the shoot even stayed in the guest house here,' says S. Kruparao, the sixty-eight-year-old pastor at a church in Uppada. 'All that is in the sea now. Even the guest house.'

The *District Census Handbook of East Godavari* published in 1961 has a reference to a guest house, too: 'There is a very comfortable Travellers Bungalow with two suites of rooms about a furlong from the sea-shore. This is said to have been built after the previous Travellers Bungalow was swallowed up by the sea.' So the guest house that the crew of *Naakuu Swatantram*...occupied is at least the second one to have vanished under the waves.

The artefacts and structures taken in by the sea often resurface in archival records and in stories passed down through generations. Older villagers remember their parents or grandparents talking about a pedda rayi, a big stone, lying submerged in the sea for many years. The 1907 gazetteer describes something similar: 'A ruin about half a mile out at sea still catches the fishermen's nets, and children hunt the beach at spring tides for coins which are occasionally washed up from what must be a submerged town.'

The ruin also finds a mention in the 1961 handbook: 'Old fisher-folk say that sailing out in their boats or catamarans for fishing, their nets or lines are often caught by the tops of buildings or trunks of trees about a mile from the shore, and that to their own knowledge the sea has been encroaching on the village.'

The hungry sea has claimed a lot more of the village since then: almost all of its beach, countless houses, at least one temple, and a mosque. Over the last decade, the waves have also ravaged a 1,463-metre-long 'geotube' built in 2010 at an estimated cost of ₹12.16 crore to protect Uppada. Geotubes are large tubular containers filled with a slurry mix of sand and water that are used in shoreline protection and land reclamation. 'In fifteen years, I have seen large boulders of around 2 square feet melt into 6-inch pebbles because of the friction of the waves,' says twenty-four-year-old D. Prasad, a part-time fisherman who has grown up in the neighbourhood.

Uppena, a Telugu film released in 2021, captures a vastly changed Uppada, with boulders and stones along what used to be the beach, attempting to protect the village from the sea. Unlike in the 1975 film, scenes capturing the village and the sea in a single frame had to settle for bird's-eye view shots, or diagonal shots, as there was barely any beach to place the camera on.

Perhaps the most vicious attack on Uppada's shoreline in recent times was by Cyclone Gulab in late September 2021, when the sea took in at least thirty houses. In December, Cyclone Jawad severely damaged the newly constructed Uppada–Kakinada road, rendering it unsafe for use.

The turbulent sea in the aftermath of Gulab took away the remnants of Maramma's old family home in early October. It also washed away the home she and her husband were living in.

⌢

'After the cyclone [Gulab] many of us were forced to sleep on the elevated platforms outside other people's homes,' Maramma's voice quivers as she recalls the devastation caused in 2021.

Since 2004, when the cyclone forced them out of their ancestral home, Maramma and her husband, T. Babai, have lived in two houses—a rented one first, and then a home of their own. Last year's cyclone tossed that home into the sea. Today, the couple live in the open on a platform outside a relative's house in the neighbourhood.

'At one point in time, we were a *"sound-party"* [credit worthy and relatively well-off],' says Maramma. The cycle of displacement and rebuilding, combined with the wedding expenses of their four daughters, have left the family's savings significantly depleted.

'We had taken loans from people to build a house, but the house got submerged,' says M. Poleshwari, from a fisher family here, echoing Maramma's anguish. 'We take debts again and the house gets submerged again.' Poleshwari has lost two houses to the sea so far. Now living in her third house, she constantly worries about her family's finances and the safety of her husband, a deep-sea fisherman. 'If there is a cyclone when he goes out, he might die. But what else can we do? The sea is our only livelihood.'

Other sources of income are also drying up. Prasad remembers how, as children, he and his friends would scout the beach during low tide to collect shells, which they would sell for some pocket money. With the sand and beach disappearing rapidly, the shells also vanished; the buyers followed suit soon enough.

'We collected these shells hoping to sell them,' Poleshwari says, looking at the old shells drying in the sun outside her house. 'People used to come here shouting "we buy shells, we buy shells"—now they rarely come.'

After the cyclone of September 2021, Maramma and around 290 others from the fishing colony wrote to Andhra Pradesh chief minister Jagan Reddy, drawing his attention to the growing danger and distress in their village. 'Earlier, Sri Y. S. Rajashekhar Reddygaru (ex-chief minister) had laid big stones along the coast of the fishing village of Uppada and saved the village from merging into the sea. These stones saved us from cyclones and tsunamis that came along,' said their letter.

'Now due to the increased number of cyclones, the large stones on the shore have been displaced and the bank is destroyed. The rope that binds the stones is also worn out. So, the houses and huts lining the shore have become one with the sea. The fishers along the coastline are living in terror,' they added, requesting that the boulders be replaced with bigger ones.

However, according to Dr Rao, there is little evidence that the boulders can provide a permanent defence against a determined sea; they are at best a makeshift remedy as the sea continues to encroach. 'Don't try to protect property. Protect the beach. The beach protects your property,' he says. And adds that 'offshore barriers in the sea like the huge stone structures which break the waves off Japan's Kaike coast—can help prevent erosion at Uppada.'

∿

Even as the sea chips away at it, the village is witnessing changes in its social makeup. In the 1980s, the weaving community—Uppada is famous for its exquisite handwoven silk saris—moved from the edge of the village to its interior parts after the government allotted them some land there. Gradually, the more affluent villagers, mainly belonging to the upper castes, also started moving further away from the sea. But the fishing community, their livelihoods inextricably linked to the sea, had no choice but to stay put.

With the upper castes escaping to safer areas, some of the customs and practices associated with the caste system began to weaken; for instance, the fishing community was no longer forced to hand over their catch, free of cost, for upper caste festivities. Slowly, the fishing community started turning to Christianity. 'Many joined the religion for their freedom,' says Kruparao, the pastor. Most people here are very poor and belong to social groups originally categorized as Backward Classes. Kruparao remembers experiencing multiple instances of caste humiliation before embracing Christianity.

'Around 20–30 years ago, most of the villagers were Hindus. The village regularly celebrated festivities for the local goddess,' says Chinnabbai's son, O. Durgayya. 'Now most of the village is Christian.' A neighbourhood that, until the 1990s, used to take its weekly off on Thursdays [to pray to the goddess], now takes Sundays off to go to church. Villagers say there were a handful of Muslims in Uppada a few decades ago, but many of them moved out after the local mosque was submerged.

For those who stay back in the village, the signs and lessons for survival come from the encroaching sea itself. '[Danger] is recognizable; the stones begin to make a peculiar *ghollughollu* sound. Earlier, we would look at the stars [to predict the pattern of the waves]; they would shine differently. Now the mobile phones tell us this,' K. Krishna, a fisherman, had told me when I met him during my first trip here in 2019. 'Sometimes, when the east wind comes from the fields, the fishermen won't even find a rupee [i.e. fish in the sea],' his wife K. Poleru added, as the three of us listened to the waves from their hut at the edge of the fishing colony. Cyclone Gulab destroyed that hut and they have since moved to a new one.

Maramma, meanwhile, continues to spend her days and nights on the platform outside her relative's house. The tremor in her voice gives away her dismay and sense of loss as she says, 'The sea has swallowed the two houses we built; I don't know if we can build another.'

DESPOTS, DISTILLERS, POETS, AND ARTISTS: CHARACTERS OF THE COUNTRYSIDE

P. Sainath

He knew an awful lot about moneylenders. He also knew how many exactly there were in town. How many held licences, how many worked freelance. But, he insisted, he was not one himself. Heaven forbid. So how did he know so much about them? Oh, that was easy. You keep your eyes and ears open. You observe, you learn.

We were in Kapil Narain Tiwari's house in Khariar. Tiwari is a leading political figure in Kalahandi. Few have fought so fiercely as he has for the rights of people there. We had wanted to talk to a town-based moneylender with rural clients. He had invited one to meet us. And the man had agreed to speak. Such is the respect Tiwari commands. All of us maintained the polite facade that our guest was not really a moneylender. He just knew a lot about them. He kept his eyes and ears open and observed and learnt.

In a selfish sense, rural India is a journalist's paradise. You'd find it hard to match its rich array of characters, for one thing. 'Characters' here does not mean just individuals, but also groups. There were people like the Manatu Mhowar (Man-eater of Manatu). That tyrannical landlord of Palamau began a meeting by politely suggesting that I throw in a lot of abuses about him in my report. 'Otherwise,' he said, 'I hope you know that your editors won't publish your story.'

Then there were the illicit distillers of Ramnad who taught us how to make arrack. Or the writer in the same district who felt that 3 a.m. was the ideal time for an interview. There were the two male poets of Pudukkottai who wrote songs of women's liberation. The hordes of small farmers who make the cockfight of Malkangiri such a unique social event. The remote village in Godda where children were trained to sing a song of welcome in English for a visiting minister who could hardly speak the language himself.

Though they are very strong individuals, all the characters here represent more than just themselves. They mirror trends, groups, even movements. Writer Ponnusamy is very individualistic indeed. Still, few can catch the flavour of Ramnad as he does in his work. Interviewing people like him was fun. But it was, above all, an education. Fire-brigade journalism—the flit-in, flit-out school—really misses out on this. It's restating the obvious, but: learning something about the area you are going to, or of the people you want to speak to helps catch that richness. Patience and the right questions help too.

After that, as our moneylender so correctly put it: you keep your eyes and ears open. You observe, you learn.

The Ex-man-eater of Manatu

DALTONGANJ, Palamau (Bihar): 'The public promoted my cheetah to a lion—thanks to journalists like you—that's why

I got such a bad image. You are interviewing me now. But I hope you know that your editors won't publish your story unless it contains a few gaalis (abuses) against me?'

Meet Jagdhishwar Jeet Singh, the Manatu Mhowar (Man-eater of Manatu). Once the most feared of the tyrannical landlords of Palamau—and perhaps of all Bihar. Also, the subject of documentaries, and of stories by the *BBC*, among a host of others. A holder of the world record for the number of bonded labour cases brought against a single person (ninety-six at one point). And a Jharkhand Party candidate who lost his deposit in the 1991 assembly polls.

The terror of the Manatu area of Palamau, the Mhowar allowed no one outside his family to construct a pucca house in his fiefdom for decades. He levied fines and taxes on villagers and ran an empire of thousands of acres on forced and bonded labour. His reputation—fully earned—was terrible. Villagers dreaded the man who kept a cheetah for a pet.

'Look, some people raise goats and some people gardens. Now goats devastate gardens, don't they? But I like to raise both gardens and goats, all creatures. I only kept a simple cheetah (it died in 1982). People say I threw peasants to it. If so, could I have let it run about free in my house, endangering my own family? But you journalists need a sensation. So my cheetah became a lion, and I a man-eater.

'You charge me with bonded labour, but we live in an era where even a man's son feels no bond to him. So how can anyone remain bonded?

'Are you taking my photograph? Get the angle right. I have to look sufficiently wicked. You'll probably have to touch it up, you know. The last journal did that—apparently I didn't look evil enough for their story.

'And let me stand for a photograph in front of my car.' The car is an ancient, decrepit-looking Dodge that has not seen the road in a long time. 'You see my wealth and splendour? Like car, like owner. Both are in the same condition.'

How does the actual record fit with such seeming simplicity? With the charm and the easy humour? Badly. Across the villages of Manatu lies a trail of bloodshed and pain. A trail of families bonded ages ago for having borrowed ₹5. Of people subjected to unspeakable terror. And of cases falling flat in court due to witnesses being too afraid to appear against the mighty one of Manatu.

But the Mhowar's downfall began in the late 70s and accelerated in the 80s. It came about more from the loss of forced and bonded labour than perhaps any other single factor. Anti-Mhowar officials and a vigorous CPI agitation in the 70s made it very difficult for him to retain bonded labour. By the late 80s, Naxalite groups had become active in his area. And today, squads of the extremist Maoist Communist Centre (MCC) stalk his domain, forcing him to spend more time in Daltonganj than in Manatu.

The actions of a block development officer, Bumbahadur Singh, put Jagdishwar Jeet Singh under a great deal of pressure in the 70s. The landlord found himself bogged down. All of a sudden, he was fighting a whole lot of cases brought against him. The charges ranged from large-scale timber smuggling to atrocities against villagers. Bumbahadur Singh also curbed the landlord's habit of trampling on the common property rights of the villagers.

'Bumbahadur? Only the first bit of his name goes well. He was anything but bahadur (brave). I defeated all his cases. They were motivated by caste and personal jealousy,' claims the landlord. (The officer was a Rajput and the Mhowar is a Bhumihar.) Nevertheless, those battles seriously eroded his position.

Why join the Jharkhand Party? 'Because they are for the poor, the oppressed and the tribals. I too am oppressed. I'm an old man (now about seventy) who has lost so much land and who just wants to live in peace. The Jharkhand Party wants a separate state and development for the adivasis. And I am for that.'

But he is hardly an adivasi? 'Don't confuse the Jharkhand Party with other Jharkhandi movements like the JMM. The Jharkhand Party sees all of us living in this region as adivasis.'

'He joined the Jharkhand Party,' says a leading businessman of Daltonganj I meet after the interview, 'because he wanted to save his land. For that, he needed some political clout. The Congress was not strong enough to help him after the 70s. And he had alienated the Janata Party and its successors.'

Jagdishwar Jeet Singh has still managed to hold on, by one estimate, to about 1,200 acres of land. That is over thirty times the legal limit. And the filthy, decaying house where I interviewed him in Daltonganj sits atop property worth ₹30 lakh. Yet, he has gone to seed. As a peep at the backyard disclosed, the 'man-eater of Manatu' is selling buffalo milk—he has a sizeable fleet of bovines there—to earn an extra buck. What explains the combination of wealth and decay?

'He has money,' says the businessman, 'but even he

knows his reign is over. This sort of landlord simply cannot make the transition to the new situation. Some feudal tyrants have made that transition cleverly. But this sort doesn't want to pay anyone anything. They have been used to terror, forced labour, and unpaid services all their lives. When these are curbed, they become pathetic. Only a part of the land with him is cultivated. If he wants to resort to forced labour, he has to contend with the Socialists, the Communists, and the MCC. So he just decays. His fangs have been drawn.'

Once a while, he still does try enforcing his writ. The Chhotanagpur Samaj Vikas Sansthan—a local NGO—had successfully overseen the distribution of some of his surplus land last year. This had gone to eighty poor families in the Pathan block who officially received pattas to that land. Even as I was interviewing the Mhowar, I am later to learn, a group close to him attacked those families. The local police, charge villagers there, are either with the landlord or seeking bribes from them. But as I am leaving Palamau, an angry deputy commissioner and the superintendent of police seem to have called the Mhowar's bluff. The poor families retain control of the land.

'Palamau,' says a local political activist, 'will prosper when the curse of people like these is removed. We have to wipe out these feudal vestiges in land and agriculture. Else, there is no future for us.' All the evidence suggests he is right.

'So you are leaving?' asked Jagdishwar Jeet Singh at the end of our interview in the morning. The man-eater who could be on his way to becoming the toothless tabby of Palamau, waved goodbye: 'Don't forget to give me those gaalis in your article. Your story won't be complete unless you throw in some abuses against me. And I can't do anything. What's the point of taking on journalists? If I take on one, the rest will start giving me gaalis.'

Hey, Hey, Hey, It's a Beautiful Day!

GODDA (Bihar): there was some cause for jubilation. The minister was not going to be more than two and a half hours late. Pretty decent punctuality by ministerial standards. Not that anybody really minded. I certainly didn't. The two tribal cultural troupes (one Santhal, one Paharia) were holding us spellbound. It made even the oppressive heat a bit more tolerable.

The sheer beauty of their skills made some of us wish the minister, Birendra Singh, wouldn't show up at all. Once he did, they would be restricted to a song each and goodbye. The over-enthusiastic vigour of the drummers had, possibly, something to do with the refreshments plied to them by a couple of stage managers a while before. At least, the stage managers referred to them as refreshments. It seemed the polite thing to do. In any case, the troupes were magnificent.

Scores of people running around and behind a retinue of cars signalled the arrival of the minister. 'Mantri aa gaya (The minister has come)' went the cry. People swiftly gathered under a shamiana to listen to the minister. 'Mantriji ka samay bahut kam hai (The minister has very little time)!' said the block development officer at least thrice over the mike. This was a message to the cultural troupes that the minister's performance required more time than their own.

After the ritual garlanding, a group of young girls from the local mission school began singing in angelic voices. In parts, their song sounded vaguely familiar. When they hit the chorus for the second time, I sat up. It couldn't be.

It was.

They were singing: *'Hey, hey, hey it's a beautiful day! Say, say, say, happy welcome to you.'*

A strange but entertaining medley of different popular songs, perhaps woven together by some mischievous priest with a sense of humour. But since these lines were sung in English, they didn't make the impact they deserved to, here in Godda, Bihar.

'Mantriji ka samay bahut kam hat,' intoned the BDO when the girls had packed it in and the boys were just about to begin. The BDO wiped the sweat off his forehead—far from being a beautiful day, it was insufferably sultry. 'Samay bahut kam hai,' he said again twice, as if afraid of forgetting the line if he didn't repeat it often enough.

Soon, he parroted his incantation over the mike and the boys finished their last two verses at a gallop. The cultural troupes stepped forward.

The political-level floor organizers had problems now. The over-excited state of the drummers had deepened. Perhaps they had had more refreshments. The drummers of one troupe mischievously rattled off practice beats as the singers of the second were belting out their welcome. However, with some deadly glares, a few whispered warnings and some deft work on the sidelines, the situation (as the BDO was later to observe) was brought under control.

Quickly, the cultural component of the day's proceedings

was brought to a close. All of it, by my count, within twenty-five minutes, perhaps even less. It had to be so. Because, as the BDO reminded us, 'Samay bahut kam hai,' and there was so much work to be done.

After the BDO concluded his signature tune, MLA Hemlal Murmu took the floor to welcome the minister. 'This isn't possible!' I exclaimed to my neighbour as Hemlal mounted the podium. 'The man's a JMM MLA and there's an all-Jharkhand bandh and blockade on. He's supposed to be blockading Birendra Singh, not welcoming him. JMM activists are being arrested not 10 kilometres from here. How can this be?'

'This is Bihar,' my neighbour said proudly. 'Besides, this is about what the blockade amounts to, anyway,' Perhaps, chipped in another member of the audience, we ought to read more into it. Hemlal had defected once, from the CPI to the JMM when he thought (correctly) that would help him win an election. Could it be that he was poised to move on again, this time to the Janata Dal?

We pondered the matter while waiting for Hemlal to begin. That took some time. His first five minutes were spent in battling, rather ineffectively, with a defective mike. A replacement mike was found and Hemlal effusively welcomed mantri mahoday. That took some time, too. Almost as much time as all the cultural troupes and performers together. When he finished, another official had his say briefly and then it was Birendra Singh's turn.

Now, as we discovered, bahut samay tha. When I left about half an hour later, he was still speaking. I withdrew, disappointed by Godda's version of the all-Jharkhand blockade.

A week later, I was treated to some blockading myself. The lodge where I had parked my stuff was raided by the police at night. An energetic, youthful, and highly suspicious deputy superintendent of police was in charge. He had just taken into custody my neighbours, a couple of 'suspicious characters' against whom the police had apparently received some tip-off.

The suspicions about their character were not without basis. They were found with equipment that possibly had some artistic uses, but is associated in the minds of the police with counterfeiters. They even confessed to having been in that trade once. But that was long ago. Now they were honest, upright citizens. They had clung on to the equipment for purely sentimental reasons. For old times' sake, as it were. But policemen, especially DSPs, are notoriously unsentimental. He was not willing to see reason.

There was no electricity during most of this period, just like during any other period in Godda. So I stumbled on the raid in darkness. The place was alive with rats and police. The first squeaked at me derisively as I mounted the stairs. The latter strode towards me decisively as I approached my room.

The DSP wanted to know: if I was (as I claimed) a journalist and had been (as I claimed) in the district so many days—then why had I not registered myself with 'the authorities'? Had I, for instance, notified his boss, the superintendent of police, of my arrival in Godda? Since I wasn't a convicted criminal on parole, nor a habitual offender on the police list, I didn't know the answer to that one.

Mercifully, for once, I had my accreditation card on me. The police left with my neighbours whom I haven't seen since—the enterprising lodge keeper immediately re-letting rooms they had booked for the next several days. He seemed to sense, shrewdly, that the police would be offering them alternative accommodation for a while.

I was tempted to go down to the station myself and have a look. But it was late, a four-day slog in the hills had exhausted me, and better sense finally prevailed. I had new neighbours, but I still occupied the same room and not a cell.

Hey, hey, hey, it's a beautiful day.

A Day at the Distillers

MUDUKULLUTHUR, Ramnad (Tamil Nadu): melt down 8 kilos of palm jaggery in a big pot. Throw in 4 kilos of kadukai (a dry fruit), a dollop of nutmeg, and a dash of poppy seed. Add the ayurvedic preparation, Carburaharasai, a finger of ginger and alum. Top off with banana skin and date fruit. Bury for a week, recover, boil, and distil. And what have you got?

Probably a conviction and a ₹500 fine. Arrack is illegal in Tamil Nadu. If you've added optionals like battery cells, chillies, and cow dung to the recipe to speed up the fermentation process, your punishment could be stiffer. His worship might wag a finger at you while raising the fine a few hundred.

This is Tamil Nadu's most widely patronized illegal industry. But who are its 'grassroots' operatives?

Finding an answer to that clearly involves talking to the distillers of illicit arrack themselves. Here, this means looking for them in the woods of Mudukulluthur in Ramnad district. After hours of what seems aimless wandering, we find them.

The meeting doesn't go quite as intended. At the sight of us, the distillers make a strong assault on existing land speed records, leaving all their equipment behind. This, it later turns out, is because I am wearing khaki trousers—symbolizing the police. Their flight does allow for calm, unhurried photographing of their abandoned apparatus, but the pictures are clearly not going to speak a thousand words. We still need to talk to them.

An hour and a couple of kilometres later, we find and pacify them. 'Why did you have to run like that when you saw us?' I ask. 'Why did you have to wear khaki trousers?' they want to know. Swamy and Kannan, our two distillers, are cheerful, courteous, and charming—and completely outrageous liars, especially on the economics of their trade. They make very little out of it, they plead.

But if this line of work is so unrewarding, why choose it? Their spiel for the next half-hour makes arrack distillation seem a virtue. They are only doing this, Swamy explains, to keep the wolf from the door.

In that, they seem to have succeeded admirably. They admit to producing up to 50 litres a day (which makes them small–medium operators). This means they can generate a turnover of around ₹1,600 daily. And Kannan seems to be wearing an expensive make of sunglasses. They never, they explain piously, use filthy stuff like battery cells, though they know others who do—their rivals in the same woods.

'We also drink what we make here,' says Swamy nobly, reminding me of similar signs about food in some Bombay restaurants.

I say I thought they had the police well in hand: then

why the record-shattering sprint when they first saw me? 'Normally, there is some cooperation,' agrees Swamy coyly. 'But this new DSP Kannappan who has come here is a terrible fellow, saar. He won't accept bribes.' While there is grudging respect for this strange policeman, they abuse a sub-inspector who 'took bribes and then beat us on orders'.

Both distillers and the look-out they've posted seem ever-ready to bolt deeper into the woods if necessary. But we meet only their wholesaler and a client so tanked up he can't tell whether he's coming or going. The client stops only a few minutes to convince us his father was a zamindar. Swamy and Kannan speak eloquently of their own humble agri-labour origins. But they are clearly better off and now prey on other agricultural workers.

Yet, at another level, both are small links in a chain that reaches to ministerial heights in this state. That is a chain of payoffs, bribes, and demands totalling crores of rupees. But these two are, relatively, small-timers. They do not enjoy a great deal of political protection. The big distillers do.

What about the ethical dimensions of their trade? For them, there are none. 'What other employment is open to us?' asks Swamy.

Arrack, both insist, is a necessity for those who do hard labour. But don't women labour more without getting into the same habits? Oh, well, women, after all, are women. There's not much that can be done about that, is there? They now shift to explaining their distribution and sale system.

All this while, the mix is boiling in a big lead pot. On top of this sits a smaller—empty—mud pot with a hole in the bottom and a tube jutting out of its side. The inside end of the tube rests on a suspended plate. Atop the mud container is an even smaller copper pot with plain water.

As the mix in the lead pot boils, the substance begins to vaporize and rise to the top of the mud pot. There it hits the copper bottom of the water container, returns, and gets distilled out through the tube into a waiting bottle. The first three bottles—they will get ten in all—contain a highly concentrated substance. When they mix these ten bottles with four bottles of water, they will get roughly ten litres of arrack.

Ramnad, among India's most backward districts, has a big list of convictions of arrack distillers. Nearly one every two hours, according to official data here. That rivals the record of Pudukkottai next door. Fine collections are also substantial: over 10 lakh rupees in the past 150 days.

The trade is huge and widespread. As in Pudukkottai, it traps a big part of the earnings of male agricultural workers addicted to arrack. Here too most women hate it as a destroyer of family income and peace.

In several villages along the coastline, many fishermen also admit to drinking a lot of arrack. Sometimes, at a cost of three-quarters of a day's earnings—daily in some seasons. Arrack merchants allow credit to those they know they have hooked.

Swamy and Kannan allow me to take photographs of the distillation process but are shy of appearing in the pictures themselves. I explain as I get up to leave—for they have never imagined anything so foolish could exist—that I am a teetotaller. Ah well, their philosophical looks seem to say as we part, it takes all sorts to make a world.

Fowl Play in Malkangiri

MALKANGIRI (Orissa): Dhanurjoy Hanthal is delighted he can speak to me in Telugu. A poor peasant knowing both that language and his native Oriya, he has run into us at the most popular social event in Malkangiri: the kukuda ladoi, or cockfight.

In a region where people can labour fourteen hours to earn less than ₹10, the cockfight is an event where thousands of rupees can change hands in minutes. Many of the fighter cocks are brought to the battleground by little peasant farmers who immediately face a barrage of bids for their birds from agents and brokers. Some of the birds sell for ₹600 to ₹800. The agents, who know a good fighter when they see one, want to buy the bird off the farmer and earn big money. They can do this by matching it against the 'appropriate' opponent. Some agents buy more than one bird.

This means the agents can sometimes select both the fighter and its rival and, to that extent, rig the outcome. They can make money both ways: from the betting the fight attracts and its actual result. No agent, however, could persuade Dhanurjoy on this day.

'He is the champion,' says Dhanurjoy proudly, cradling a cantankerous looking white cock in his arms. 'He will just destroy his opponent. Lay your money on him.' Dhanurjoy is shouting to make himself heard. Samosa vendors, makeshift tea stall owners, jalebi makers and biscuit sellers have shown up at this odd venue a few kilometres from Malkangiri town to hawk their stuff at the top of their voices.

And then there are the birds.

We could hear them from nearly a kilometre away across the plain. Piercing, hair-raising shrieks of aggression hit the air as they worked themselves up into a rage before the fight. The venue is a sea of strange colours. An arena crammed with battling broilers of different hues, each bird tied, comically, by a thin string to a little clump of grass.

Villainous white cocks hurl abuse at rowdy red ones. Huge black birds spit fowl expletives at their spotted challengers. Even from a distance, it sounds as if heated debates have led to violence at an all-India poultry convention. And still more men are coming, many with blindfolded birds in their arms, walking single file down different pathways from the hills. Farmers themselves, they move respectfully in lines along the ridges dividing the plots of cultivated land to avoid trampling on crops. Some have come all the way from neighbouring Andhra Pradesh. We are now standing in the middle of the bowl of land they are converging on. From here, the lines of people from the hills make a spectacular sight.

Already in Malkangiri we have seen trainers put birds through their paces very early in the morning. It's a bit disconcerting to step into a street in that tiny town and watch a cock being tossed over a wall or other barrier. 'They have to learn to leap with force and anger,' explained Anand, one of the trainers. There was also Krishna Reddy, who had turned up just for the coming big fight, his blindfolded bird screeching in rage at unseen enemies around 5 a.m. in the morning. From them, we had learnt of the main event and its venue. When we left, the birds in training were still learning to leap with force and anger.

At the venue, the event takes its time getting started. The matching of the birds and the leech-like persistence of the agents and brokers delays proceedings. Finally, loud cries announce the fixing of a couple of bouts. Now the bets are on. 'Das rupya rengda, bees rupya dabbla (ten on the red, twenty on the white),' and so it goes—upwards. Among those accepting bets is a respectable-looking, elderly gentleman of enormous dignity. Dhanurjoy tells me he is the headmaster of a school in the vicinity.

The kukuda ladoi has been a Malkangiri tradition for centuries. Gambling has always been a part of it, though many poor peasants enter for the love of the battle. But in the last few decades, commerce has crept in. Now, owners attach frighteningly sharp, narrow knives to the feet of the birds, to speed up the combat and ensure swift results.

This cruel feature has transformed the traditional cockfight. Earlier, a single bout could last an hour or more, with the contestants rambling all over the area. With the knives, it's all over in minutes. Dhanurjoy shows us five pairs of knives, explaining how his champion will change his footwear for each fight, depending on the capability and size of his rival. Clearly, the bird has a long day ahead.

The ring is about 25 feet in diameter, creatively constructed from twigs and bamboo sticks. The organizer gets an entry fee from each bird owner. Also, a percentage on everything, from the bets to a liberal share of the blows during any fist fight. This one allows me the privilege of taking photographs from within the ring.

First come the flyweights. The heavier birds are reserved for later when both crowd and betting are at their highest.

The opening bout closes almost immediately. A white cock, pitted against a red, bolts the ring and shoots off across the countryside. Its owner moans in despair. In kukuda ladoi the defeated bird's master loses not only his money, but also the bird—which ends up as the rival owner's dinner.

Once the flyweights are out of the way, the middles take possession of the ring for a while. The fights begin with the owners of the two birds holding the contestants in their arms and swinging them thrice towards each other, beak-to-beak. This, apparently, is a way of getting the fighters acquainted with their antagonists. A sort of squaring-off, allowing each a quick opportunity of sizing up its combatant. After the third swing, they seemingly begin a fourth, but this time fling the cocks at each other in mid-air. With that, the bout is on.

Not always so, though. As we learn at the training sessions, cocks are curious of temperament. One moment, their rage is terrible, completely focused on annihilating the rival. The next, it is seemingly spent—and then back again a minute later. We watched two birds outside the tea stall in the morning. They were pecking at something or the other peacefully, in the usual manner of their kind. Suddenly, they would look up at each other and charge into combat uttering hideous oaths. For a few moments there would be a flurry of feathers while we held our breath. Then, equally suddenly, almost on an invisible, inaudible signal, they would break off and go about pecking for food peaceably. Next, without warning, but perfectly synchronized, came blistering bird blasphemies as they charged one another yet again at tremendous speed. This leisurely war and peace scenario continued for nearly half an hour.

Here, at the event, they are allowed no such luxuries. This the real thing. Once the birds are thrown at each other, the masters circle around them as they fight, now encouraging, now abusing, hurling them back into the fray if they break off for too long.

Dhanurjoy's big moment comes after a few more bouts when his white champion is matched against a ruffianly red rooster. Even as the owners swing the two birds beak to beak, allowing them to size each other up, the red cock catches Dhanurjoy's bird a deadly if unscrupulous blow on the neck. An impartial referee would stop the bout at this point. But the man who could have been that is busy counting the gate receipts, which are mounting satisfactorily. With the result that Dhanurjoy's champion goes woozily into:

Round one: the birds move their ungainly feet with unsuspected speed, agility, and power. But our champion is clearly off colour. The Red Menace comes in, firing on all fronts, his deliberately sharpened beak and the knives on his feet traumatizing Dhanurjoy's Great White Hope.

The champ takes at least four ugly nicks on the breast and under the wings. The audience is hysterical. But the knives on the birds' feet are coming loose, so the owners enforce a temporary truce to retie them. This allows the contestants a minor respite before:

Round Two: both birds shoot into the air, ripping away relentlessly. Dhanurjoy's champion, still smarting from the early blow, is just a fraction of a second slower. It is a fatal fraction of a second. His rival rips upwards as he lands, cutting into the neck. The Red Menace then closes in for the kill.

184

Two razor-sharp jerks draw bloody patches on the white one's breast.

At this point, the white cock turns philosophical. Almost as if there was no such thing as a fight on, he strolls off to a corner and sits down to meditate, oblivious to the jeers of an unsympathetic crowd, unmindful of his master's admonishments. His mind seems occupied by higher matters, such as how to leave the ring alive.

While he takes the count, Dhanurjoy addresses his charge in language that would not be tolerated in the state legislature. I see him again later, the limp champion in his hand. It is hard to say who looks more crestfallen, farmer or fowl. Most of the subsequent winners too are reds and blacks. It is a bad day for White supremacists.

Krishna Reddy, whose red rooster is among the victors, tells us there is a cockfight almost every day of the week in some part of the district. Some of these draw even larger crowds, he says. The season begins around October and ends in February.

The light is now too poor for photography, and my flash is behaving badly. As we leave, the bets have multiplied by several times, the crowd and noise become unbelievable. Many of those we have spoken to, such as Madhaba Gonda, Vasant Pinki, or Krishna Reddy, have been to cockfights for over a decade.

We pass Dhanurjoy on the way out, his hands empty, knives dangling unused by his side, as he trudges towards his village, beaten but not broken. There shall, after all, be another day, another bird, another bout, another bet.

Minstrels with a Mission

PUDUKKOTTAI (Tamil Nadu): one is a schoolteacher. The other, a Life Insurance Corporation (LIC) officer. Both are thirty-seven years old and male. Sounds very commonplace. Yet Jayachandar and Muthu Bhaskaran are hardly that. They must rank as an unusual pair in any setting, rural or urban.

Each is an independent songwriter. Both write highly popular songs in Tamil. They often aim their lyrics specifically at women—urging them to stand up for their rights, to rebel. The songs call on women to realize their potential and to prove they are every inch as capable as men, if not more so. Of course, they have written songs on other subjects, but what's striking is the way women in Tamil Nadu's least urbanized district have responded to their songs.

And it's strong stuff: 'Never get entangled in the words of those who say "it's impossible for women"' go the lines of one Jayachandar song. 'Dispel these illusions...throw fire on the atrocities they threaten you with. Like a bird with wings clipped, society has enslaved you within the home. Now come out like a gathering storm.'

Muthu Bhaskaran's song, 'O sister, come learn cycling, move with the wheel of time' has proved a classic. Almost every female neo-literate, neo-cyclist here has sung or knows of this song. A sample line: 'The men are riding the cycles with the women on the carriers? That's an old story, sister. Let's rewrite it now with you in the driver's seat.' In a district where women have taken to cycling in astonishing numbers as part of the literacy drive, the popularity and impact of this song is immeasurable. But it has gone beyond

Pudukkottai too. The song has been translated into Hindi, Telugu, Kannada, and Malayalam.

Jayachandar's songs also are now sung in more than one language. The fame of both poets has gone beyond this obscure, backward district. Jayachandar revels in the curious pseudonym Vettri Nilavan, or 'Moon of Victory'. The last time I met him, he had just returned from Coimbatore where he had gone to record a pro-literacy song aimed at that city's textile workers. And there are other themes. 'Human Once Again' is the title of one of his anti-liquor songs. Its protagonist is a reformed alcoholic.

The pro-literacy songs go beyond advocacy of the ABCs: 'Things won't change simply because we say so...we have to fight in many ways...and one of these is learning' goes one of his numbers. 'The mighty hands, that plough the lands, and pluck the weeds, now take the lamp, the light of knowledge... and drive away the darkness of illiteracy...change your life... if we learn to read and write we can't be cheated any more.'

'So what if a female child is born' goes another popular Jayachandar song, written after the poet was moved by reports of female infanticide. 'Keep aside, and take your mourning with you. Is there any world without women? Give me an answer.'

It's much more powerful in Tamil, of course. Between them, the two have written over fifty songs. These are on literacy, against arrack, for advancing women's rights, and promoting science and scientific thinking. And people are listening. In large numbers.

Muthu Bhaskaran, an MA in Tamil from Madurai University, is a teacher at the Government Model Higher

Secondary School. Jayachandar, a BSc in mathematics and from a family of agriculturists, works in the LIC. What was the turning point in their thinking? Both speak of their participation in the 'East Coast Jatha'. That was a march from Pondicherry to Kanyakumari in the late 80s. 'It was my first exposure to a scientific literacy campaign,' says Jayachandar.

Both also gained from their contact with the Tamil Nadu Science Forum and the Progressive Writers Association. And both were deeply moved by their work in and interaction with the literacy movement, Arivoli Iyakkam, in their own district. 'I noticed changes within me and as society changed me, I thought I would try to change society,' says Muthu Bhaskaran. Before his Arivoli experience, he says, 'I thought of women in the old way, that they can't really come out and do things. But in Arivoli, I have learned very different. Given the chance, there is nothing they cannot achieve.'

How do men react to songs asking women to call their bluff? 'Why men?' laughs Muthu Bhaskaran, 'some mocking from them was inevitable, but a few of the older women too were scandalized. However, girls in the 15–25 age group picked up the songs very quickly.'

Has either ever had reason to look back and find that events have overtaken one of his songs? 'Yes,' says Muthu Bhaskaran. I felt that way after watching an eight or nine-year-old Harijan girl weave wonderful circles on a cycle late at night in the near darkness of Ambedkar Nagar village. So I wrote an on-the-spot sequel to my earlier song. Thus begins: "Yes, brother, I have learnt cycling. I'm moving with the wheel of time...."'

Valia the Honest Chowkidar

PETLAWAD, Jhabua (M. P.): 'My policy is very clear. I am not paid to be a hero. For what we are paid, we need do nothing. Yet, I do try and stop group clashes in the village. I try my best. Should we stick our necks out to do what the police are paid for but fail to do? Raat ka jhagda, subah jayenge (a clash in the night, we look at it in the morning). Then we act.'

Valia Deva Katara is the lowest functionary, the last link in the mighty apparatus of state. He is paid by the revenue department, but reports to the police. His immediate boss is the patwari. Valia is a village chowkidar or kotwar (spelt kotwal in some states). Officials describe him as the smallest unit of the police in India. But that is not a description he relishes. He prefers to distance himself from the police. And Valia is a modest soul. This Bhil tribal's record in stopping intra-village clashes is really quite good. That, too, in a high crime region where people can resort to violence very fast.

The village chowkidar is also the most poorly paid and least looked after minion of the state. He might not be paid in cash at all. The government could just give him a few acres of land to till. This would be only for the duration of his tenure. The land would then revert to the state. He gets no pension, no provident fund, just two dresses, one shirt and a cap. If the government is in a generous mood, he might even get a pair of shoes. Until Valia led his fellow kotwars in revolt, those given land received salaries as low as ₹18 a month. The rest got close to ₹40.

Fed up with those conditions and constant ill-treatment, he formed the Zilla Kotwar Union twelve years ago. It was probably the first of its kind in the country. All did not join, but a few score did. Their fight, against huge odds, saw the trend catch on. Chowkidars in other districts formed their own unions. Then came joint action. This culminated, five years ago, in the kotwars being paid ₹500 a month if they took no land.

Even that came after many rounds of battle. 'The salary went from ₹40 to ₹50 to ₹100 and finally to ₹500,' says Valia. 'It took many years to get that far. Most of the other conditions of work have not changed, really.' Even if given just the daily minimum wage in Madhya Pradesh, the kotwars would get at least ₹900 a month. The most any kotwar seems to have studied is up to Class VIII. Valia is a self-educated man.

Organizing the chowkidars was not easy. It still isn't. 'The nature of our jobs means that each of us gets tied down to his village. And your nearest friend is a village away. So when the kotwar goes back to his village, he is isolated and at the mercy of his bosses.' But the persistence paid off. The kotwars fought officialdom's attempts to browbeat them. They took marches to Indore and twice to Bhopal itself. It was in Indore that they met CITU leaders who first helped organize their unions and actions. 'That's how we got the ₹500 a month,' says Valia.

I first met Valia in Petlawad block HQ, a little away from his base in Bamnia. I also met kotwars from other parts of Jhabua district. 'Valia?' asked one kotwar in a village in Jhobat. 'That man is too honest. I think we need far more strong-arm tactics to get a better deal.' But he respects Valia.

'He was the first to tell the government what they could do with their land,' he said.

Valia is amused when I tell him about that. 'You only have to see the kind of land they give us to know why,' he laughs. He and his nine-member family have 5 acres of their own. Another chowkidar, Giridhar Dev, told me in Thandla block: 'Valia at least tries to stop group clashes. Most of us are not stupid enough to do that. Especially when a clash is just exploding. Why go to the village and invite both sides to target you? Don't wave a stick unless you are sure you can use it.' Babulal, chowkidar in a Petiawad village, agreed. 'Once I see them (village clans) getting ready for battle—that's when I visit my relatives in a nearby village.'

It may not be Valia's way. But the others have a point too. Valia himself concedes that. The kotwar's job does not end with maintaining the register of births and deaths. He has other, semi-police functions as well. He reports the arrival of 'new' or 'suspicious' characters in a village to the police station. 'The chowkidar is seen by the villagers as a police agent,' says Valia. 'At the same time, the police suspect his loyalty lies with the clans in his village. So he can get beaten up by either side. Sometimes by both.'

Valia's policy when a clash seems to be brewing is simple. 'There was a dispute between two groups in my village just this week. I met both groups—together. (After a while that could be impossible.) I tried hard to work out a settlement but failed. So I went to the police thana. But I took both groups with me. They took up their dispute there. I am out of it. One thing is crucial. Both groups must be present during all your efforts.' Valia may not know it, but he is adopting the 'transparency' that so many top functionaries of state preach but seldom practise.

'At our level,' says Valia when I put this to him, 'there is a compelling reason to be honest. The likelihood of violence from those who perceive themselves as being cheated by you is very high. (Jhabua has one of the highest homicide rates in India, say jail officials in Alirajpore town.) Whatever happens, one party is going to get angry with me. So I do my best to curb doubts about my own role.'

There is corruption among the chowkidars, he says. Wouldn't there be with the kind of deal they get? Some kotwars also seek safety by aligning with the police and bullying the odd villager. 'Yet, remember,' he says, 'this is Bhil territory. If you take money and can't deliver, you are in big trouble. Is a little extra money worth your life?' Those are not the only problems. Giridhar Dev pointed to other hassles of the four sabse chotta jaanwar' (the smallest animal of all). The patwari ill treats us. The tehsildar and his flunkeys harass us. The SDO bullies us. Every small havaldar pushes us around.'

'Last week,' said Babulal, 'the tehsildar came by. I was ordered to go and fetch a chicken and cook it for him. So I did that. I also waited on him hand and foot. There are no working hours for us. We are up at all hours for every small despot who arrives. Later, they threw ₹15 at me for the chicken. It was worth at least ₹50 if not more. The man I took that chicken from has a violent temper. How can I explain it to him? Now he hates me and one day will do me some damage.'

Many of the kotwars I met echoed this complaint. Much of their time went in catering to the whims of visiting petty dignitaries. What if the slave labour of the kotwars fails to please such small officials? 'Then the patwari suspends us,' said Giridhar. 'Anyway, they suspend us frequently.' That has happened to Valia too. And more than once. 'They can't reach any lower than us. We are the final scapegoats for all ills,' says he.

'In bad situations,' said one kotwar, 'we are supposed to help the police in night patrolling. They never come, but you have to patrol. If they come at all, it is at safe hours to give us orders. The risks are all ours.'

'I am getting old now,' says Valia. (He is over fifty.) 'A younger man will have to take the reins. We are in a bit of disarray now.' His tiredness and their logistical headaches have posed many problems for the unions in recent years. Valia has, in fact, put in his resignation from the kotwar's post. The patwari had sent him a rude letter demanding that he present himself in a few hours or face the sack. But when Valia resigned, the patwari didn't accept it. 'It's a joke,' says Valia. 'They sack me three times a year. But they won't let us go, finally. Where will they find such cheap labour to perform such a high risk job?'

Note: The names of the kotwars (other than Valia) in this report are not real. The names of their villages have been held back altogether. As they put it: 'Officials have a way of reaching back to the sabse chotta jaanwar and hurting them.'

The Writer and the Village

MELANMARAI NADU, Kamrajar (Tamil Nadu): he dropped out of school in the fifth standard. Some of his short stories are now required reading at the university level. But irony, always a strong point of Melanmai Ponnusamy's writing, dogs him all the way. Those stories are read at the university level in other districts. His beloved Ramnad does not have a single university of its own.

I first saw him when he was addressing a public meeting late one evening at a crowded hall in Pudukkottai. Leaning forward against a table, Ponnusamy told his audience of the dramatic impact of the Gulf War on his little Ramnad village. Some farmers there thought they had figured out their 'modernization', tractors and all. Then the war began. The steep rise in the prices of petrol, diesel, and imported components shattered their plans.

At this point, the electricity in the hall went off. Ponnusamy didn't pause for a moment. He got onto the table and went on with his speech. Nor, after the initial noise, did the audience budge. They remained spellbound in the darkness.

That was a month ago. Now we are likely to hear him in darkness again. We have spent hours searching for his lonely village and it is almost 2 a.m. when we arrive. I have broken a foot en route and the pain is at its peak. While the dogs rouse everybody for miles around, we apologize profusely for waking him up at this hour.

He seems surprised: 'Isn't this the best time to have a discussion?' he asks. Moments later, we are deep in one.

Apart from being a highly regarded writer, Ponnusamy is also, in some ways, one of the great experts on the backwardness of this district. His isolated little village, Melanmarai Nadu, is now in Kamrajar district after the division of Ramnad. From here, he chums out insights into why Ramnad remains the

194

way it does. Every story he has written in the past twenty-one years is about and located in Ramnad.

Though a Kalki Prize-winning writer and a leading figure in the Progressive Writers Association, Ponnusamy prefers to live in his cut-off village. Why not move to a big city? 'That would harm the integrity of the writing,' says he. So he remains in Melanmarai Nadu. A place so difficult to find that I arrived six hours late for our appointment.

'You're going to interview me as an expert on Ramnad's poverty? Not as a writer?' Ponnusamy clearly finds that entertaining.

'Ramanathapuram district was formed in 1910,' says Ponnusamy. 'To this day it does not have a university of its own. It has now given birth to three districts and two ministers but not a single medical college.' Nor a government engineering college. And the one private engineering institution here might wind up this year. There are just three colleges of any sort across the new district and only two postgraduate courses offered at these.

'Backwardness breeds its own mindset,' says Ponnusamy. 'There has hardly ever been even a demand for a university in Ramnad. Only in the recent past have political parties begun to speak about it. Accepting basic education is going to take a couple of generations here.

'Making demands and petitions didn't come easy to the people of Ramnad. For eighty-three years, the district headquarters was located in another district, in Madurai! Even our law courts were located in that town till just six months ago. Only with the division of Ramnad into three districts in 1985 did that change.'

This means, says Ponnusamy—who calls himself an unrepentant leftist—'that the administration has always been distanced from the people. Officials were so far away, they knew little of local issues. The area's complexity was not understood. Now we have the courts, collectorate, and other structures. Even so, the old pattern prevails because basic issues have not been touched.'

The district is among the lowest in the state in terms of income and, as a rule, lags behind the rest of Tamil Nadu by about 20 per cent on that score. This is an ex-zamindari area. It really consisted of many small fiefdoms or principalities, mostly run on a caste basis. The extent to which caste has contributed to backwardness here is enormous.'

The British period unsettled even that way of life. It destroyed the few avenues that existed for employment and income. 'A large number of people took to illegal activities. They were left with few other means of survival.' To this day, Ramnad has a very high level of violence, mainly caste-based, and of crime.

'Land reform here, of course, has been meaningless. Contrary to common belief, this district does have good agricultural potential. But who has ever worked with that view in mind?' More than 80 per cent of landholdings in Ramnad are less than 2 acres in size and uneconomical for many reasons. At the top of the list is a lack of irrigation.

'Employment and the nature of employment mould such a great part of the human character. If you have a cement factory, you have not just cement, but jobs, of a certain character. But first you need to find the location and the resources to set up such a factory. There has never been a real mapping of Ramnad's resources. And no steps ever taken to create employment of an enduring nature.'

Ponnusamy has a point. Ramnad has perhaps the lowest proportion of 'economically active population around the year', less than 40 per cent. This means a very large number of people are really scraping a living off odd jobs in most months. 'On the one hand, agriculture has failed because of poor harnessing of water resources. On the other there is no industrial development. In short, no 'consciousness-generating employment'. Productivity per worker lags behind the state's average by about 20 per cent.

Ramnad has also always had a predominance of economically weaker sections. Scheduled castes and tribes make up close to 20 per cent of its people. Besides, the district has a very high proportion of backward classes. Unemployment levels, among the worst in the state, are highest among these sections. 'We also have some of the most exploitative relationships in this district.'

Whether it is the unique Ramnad moneylender or the sorrow of the chilli farmer, Melanmai Ponnusamy has chronicled it all. Recurring drought, long-term migration or the effects of joblessness—very little escapes him. And the insights he has gained looking from down-up, just from his little village, can be startling. Often they match the results of the best research.

'New types of seeds are being used by the chilli farmers. I do not know where exactly they have come from, but they are distorting the farmer's economy. These seeds may temporarily yield more. But they also compel farmers to spend more and more on fertilisers and agro-chemicals. They are killing the land. The yield begins to fall after a while. The cost of production is now much higher for those who have begun to use these seeds.'

All his six collections of short stories and his single novel, however, reflect an irrepressible optimism. (One collection is titled *Humanity Will Win.*) 'The people here have a fighting spirit and they will change Ramnad themselves. But we cannot be complacent. We have to work for that.' And will he meanwhile continue to write only on Ramnad?

'I must be true to my writing. 'Simply by being very honest to the realities of this village, I might be producing something relevant to the reality of a village in Uttar Pradesh. It depends on whose problems you address, doesn't it?'

The Art of Pema Fatiah

BHABRA, Jhabua (M.P.): 'The havaldar was sitting there, looking over my shoulder, saab. How can one paint under such conditions? He would keep telling me, "Pema, do a good job or bada saab will be angry." Can one work under supervision of the police? My hand stops and it shakes in fear. This happened to me many times.'

His paintings have been on display in London, Rome, and other parts of the world. People pay the price of admission to see them in Bharat Bhavan, Bhopal. He has twice won state awards for art in Madhya Pradesh. Several of his works decorate the walls of senior government officers. But Pema Fatiah, perhaps the foremost exponent of the Bhil art of 'Pithora', now lives in penury. Recovering from a paralytic stroke at his home in Bhabra village of Bhabra block here, the Bhil tribal is struggling to regain his prowess. The stroke affected his painting arm.

The Pithora painting can vary in size, but is usually large. The artist mostly does his painting directly on walls. Some of Pema's works are grand murals. The Pithora is a tribal world picture. Everything the Bhil sees, senses or experiences is captured here. The horse, central to Bhil mythology, figures prominently. But figures less connected with mythology also appear. The moneylender, for instance. Or, often, the police thanedar. Both are very major realities in the lives of the Bhil tribals. You can also suddenly come across a motorcycle or an aeroplane in one of these paintings. Pema may be among the best but is by no means a lone representative of the art. Many creative artists across this region produce works that really delight.

But the Pithora is more than just a form of traditional painting, says Dr Amita Baviskar of the Delhi School of Economics. She is a scholar who has worked among communities in this area. The Pithora has a ritual context, she says. And that is a deeply religious one. The painting usually comes up as part of a religious ceremony or puja. The artist while working is said to be possessed. The gods are speaking through him. When the painting is done, the pujari will scrutinise the work to see if the essence of what the gods are saying has been captured. The Pithora draws its authenticity from its sacred character.'

Pema was trained by his father in a line he says is a hereditary occupation. Quite a few of the materials that go into his work, he makes himself. Some of the pastes and colours come from oxides, minerals, fruit and other substances locally available. He still has to buy a few materials, though.

Some of Pema's murals are stunning. One that hangs in the Jhabua collectorate (done on cloth), for instance. Even more appealing are the traditional works he has done directly on walls in his area. One was not less than eighty square feet in size. Its colours seemed almost luminous. The work itself captured a mix of myth and daily life. Alongside the horses were wells, a pump, a motorbike surrounded by snakes, a policeman. Green, red, brown, and patches of white seemed to change hue as the angle of sunlight shifted. Here, the gods of painting, at least, had spoken.

'That one was done when I was well and enjoyed my work,' says Pema. So how did it come about that he ceased to enjoy it?

Pema was first discovered—outside his own societal context—by R. Gopalakrishnan, collector of Jhabua in the mid-80s. Astonished by the quality of his work, the officer commissioned Pema to do a painting for the Collectorate. He paid him ₹5,000 for it, a huge sum in those days and the first time Pema was getting anything like it. (For his work, locally, he got payments in kind, and sometimes a little cash.) It was also perhaps the last time he got paid that way in Jhabua.

Gopalakrishnan had Pema's work displayed in Bhopal. There, it won the artist his two state awards. It also caught the attention of many leading artists, including J. Swaminathan. Pema's work was now widely exhibited. The artist remembers that part of his experience with relish. Gopalakrishnan and Swaminathan are the only individuals from that world he remembers fondly. He was really pained to learn from us that Swaminathan was no more. With that painter, perhaps, Pema struck an artist-to-artist connection. Of the officer, he says: 'Gopal saab was very good to me.'

Gopal saab himself is not so sure. He is now secretary to the chief minister of Madhya Pradesh. 'If I knew what was to happen to him subsequently,' he says ruefully, 'I do not know how I would have gone about it. The man was a genius. I did not expect the events that followed.' All that he had intended was that a great artist get the recognition due to him.

Pema's problems began when Gopalakrishnan left the district. He now had recognition, but no protection. A large number of officials, high and low, began to force paintings out of him. 'The havaldar would come and tell me, saab is calling you,' he says. 'And I went. It could be one of many saabs. The SP, the DSP, the SDM or even the tehsildar.' And so, Pema Fatiah worked, sometimes with a havaldar or some other flunkey keeping an eye on him. 'Sometimes, they would give me a little money. Sometimes, I paid for that work out of my own pocket,' he says. Pema was now working for a bunch of gods very different from his own.

Soon the pressure of this got too much for Pema to bear. As his fame grew, so did his misery. His visits to Bhopal were a sort of release. At the same time, he ended up doing even more paintings that he never got paid for. For a Gopalakrishnan, to whom he mattered as a person, Pema was a great artist. For many others, he was just a peasant producing something of value. Perhaps a work that could be profitably sold in the future. For the policeman overseeing his work in Jhabua, he was just a contemptible adivasi who produced something his bosses wanted. 'Pema's story is a good example of how an urban elite can appropriate tribal art,' says Gopalakrishnan. His work was torn from its roots, robbed of its context. Under this pressure, Pema became an alcoholic.

Finally, he cracked. He had a bad fall while on tour. This came towards the end of a night when he had drunk quite a bit. That was in November 1993, around Diwali time, he recalls. 'The next morning, I woke up and found my right hand paralysed. I was really frightened.' The stroke also affected his speech. He returned home immediately. He soon found he could do no other work either.

Learning of his tragedy, Gopalakrishnan arranged for the government to bear his medical expenses. These ran to over ₹20,000. The officer also found a job for him in the Bharat Bhavan. 'But,' says Pema, 'I could not take it up in my condition.'

When I first met Pema Fatiah in Bhabra, Meerza Ismail Beg, a retired teacher from Indore—himself an artist—was with me. The depth of Pema's knowledge and the simple way he explained his craft to us held us spellbound. His wife proudly posed by her husband when we took photographs, though she would not raise her veil until his elder brother was out of the way. She clearly knew her husband was a great talent, a great painter whose fame went far beyond Bhabra.

Now, meeting him a month later, I find Pema exercising his right arm. 'I think it might heal in time,' he says. He holds my elbow and directs me to a nearby house to show me the work he is attempting. 'It helps me to try and paint,' he says. It is not Pema at his best, but it is, at least, a fresh start. Perhaps one day the art of Pema Fatiah will work for his own gods again.

ACKNOWLEDGEMENTS

Grateful acknowledgement is made to the following copyright holders for permission to reprint copyrighted material in this volume.

'The Blue Umbrella' by Ruskin Bond. Reprinted by permission of Rupa Publications India and the author.

'Countless Hitlers' by Vijaydan Detha, translated by Christi A. Merrill and Kailash Kabir. Reprinted by permission of Kailash Kabir.

'Seed' by Mahasweta Devi, translated by Ipsita Chanda. Reprinted by permission of Seagull Books.

'Coinsanv's Cattle' by Damodar Mauzo, translated by Xavier Cota. Reprinted by permission of the author and the translator.

'The Hanging' by O. V. Vijayan, translated by A. J. Thomas. Reprinted by permission of DC Books and the translator.

'My Idea of Village Swaraj' contains excerpts from *Harijan* by Mohandas Karamchand Gandhi. These excerpts are in the public domain.

'The Village as the Nation: Making of the Indian Common Sense' was originally published in *The Indian Village: Rural Lives in the 21st Century* by Surinder S. Jodhka. Excerpt reprinted by permission of the author and the publisher.

'The Rat's Guide' was originally published in *A Matter of Rats: A Short Biography of Patna* by Amitava Kumar. Excerpt reprinted by permission of the author and the publisher.

'Oh, that house? It's in the sea now—there!' by Rahul M. was originally published in the People's Rural Archive of India on 28 Feb 2022. Reprinted by permission of the author and People's Archive of Rural India. Available at ruralindiaonline. org/en/articles/oh-that-house-thats-in-the-sea-now-there.

'Despots, Distillers, Poets and Artists: Characters of the Countryside' was originally published in *Everyone Loves a Good Drought: Stories from India's Poorest Districts* by P. Sainath. Excerpt reprinted by permission of Penguin Random House, India.

NOTES

THE INDIAN VILLAGE

1. 2011 Census of India, Office of the Registrar General and Census Commissioner of India, Government of India, 2011.
2. Ibid.

MY IDEA OF VILLAGE SWARAJ

All the excerpts are taken from *Harijan*, a magazine founded by Mohandas Karamchand Gandhi in 1933.

THE VILLAGE AS THE NATION: MAKING OF THE INDIAN COMMON SENSE

This excerpt is taken from *The Indian Village: Rural Lives in the 21st Century* by Surinder S. Jodhka, published by Aleph Book Company in 2023.

1. Ronald Inden, 'Orientalist Constructions of India', *Modern Asian Studies*, Vol. 20 (3), 1986, pp. 401–46.
2. Gurminder K. Bhambra, *Rethinking Modernity: Postcolonialism and the Sociological Imaginations*, New York: Palgrave, 2007.
3. Quoted in Surinder S. Jodhka, 'Nation and Village: Images of Rural India in Gandhi, Nehru and Ambedkar', *Economic and Political Weekly*, Vol. 37, No. 32, August, 2002, p. 3343.
4. M. N. Srinivas, 'The Indian Village: Myth and Reality', Vandana Madan (ed.) *The Indian Village*, Delhi: Oxford University Press, 1987/2002, p. 57.
5. M. K. Gandhi, *The Collected Works of Mahatma Gandhi*, Volume I, New Delhi: Government of India, 1958, p. 14.

6. Ibid., pp. 94–95.
7. J. A. Parel (ed.), *Hind Swaraj and Other Writings*, Cambridge: Cambridge University Press, 1997, p. xlii.
8. M. K. Gandhi, *The Collected Works of Mahatma Gandhi*, Volume XI, Delhi: Government of India, 1963, p. 509.
9. M. K. Gandhi, *The Collected Works of Mahatma Gandhi*, Volume XXI, Delhi: Government of India, 1966, pp. 288–89.
10. M. K. Gandhi, *The Collected Works of Mahatma Gandhi*, Volume LXXXVI, Delhi: Government of India, 1982, p. 232.
11. M. K. Gandhi, *The Collected Works of Mahatma Gandhi*, Volume LXVIII, Delhi: Government of India, 1977, p. 369.
12. M. K. Gandhi, *The Collected Works of Mahatma Gandhi*, Volume XXXIII, Delhi: Government of India, 1969, p. 151.
13. A. T. Embree, *Imagining India: Essays on Indian History*, Delhi: Oxford University Press, 1989, p. 165.
14. S. Khilnani, *The Idea of India*, New York: Farrar Straus Giroux, 1998, p. 125.
15. M. K. Gandhi, *The Collected Works of Mahatma Gandhi*, Volume LXXI, Delhi: Government of India, 1978, p. 4.
16. M. K. Gandhi, *The Collected Works of Mahatma Gandhi*, Volume LIX, Delhi: Government of India, 1974, p. 409.
17. M. K. Gandhi, *The Collected Works of Mahatma Gandhi*, Volume LXIV, Delhi: Government of India, 1976, pp. 116–17.
18. Ibid., pp. 409–10.
19. M. K. Gandhi, *The Collected Works of Mahatma Gandhi*, Volume LI, Delhi: Government of India, 1972, p. 406.
20. Ibid.
21. M. K. Gandhi, *The Collected Works of Mahatma Gandhi*, Volume XLI, Delhi: Government of India, 1970, p. 445.
22. M. K. Gandhi, *The Collected Works of Mahatma Gandhi*, Volume XXXIII, Delhi: Government of India, 1969, p. 76.
23. M. K. Gandhi, *The Collected Works of Mahatma Gandhi*,

Volume LXXVII, Delhi: Government of India, 1979, p. 228.

24. M. K. Gandhi, *The Collected Works of Mahatma Gandhi*, Volume LXXVI, Delhi: Government of India, 1979, pp. 308–09.

25. M. K. Gandhi, *The Collected Works of Mahatma Gandhi*, Volume LXII, Delhi: Government of India, 1975, pp. 319–20.

26. Jawaharlal Nehru, *An Autobiography*, Delhi: Oxford University Press, 1980 (first published 1936), p. 49.

27. Ibid., p. 52.

28. Jawaharlal Nehru, *The Discovery of India*, New York: The John Day Company, 1946, p. 244.

29. Ibid., p. 248.

30. Ibid., p. 246.

31. Ibid.

32. Ibid., p. 252.

33. Nehru, *The Discovery of India*, p. 254.

34. Nehru, *An Autobiography*, p. 52.

35. S. Gopal, *Selected Works of Jawaharlal Nehru*, Vol. 5 (Old Series), Hyderabad: Orient Longman, 1973, p. 82.

36. Nehru, *An Autobiography*, p. 52.

37. Nehru, *The Discovery of India*, p. 246.

38. S. Gopal, *Selected Works of Jawaharlal Nehru*, Vol. 3 (Old Series), Hyderabad: Orient Longman, 1972, p. 365.

39. Nehru, *An Autobiography*, p. 306.

40. Gopal, *Selected Works of Jawaharlal Nehru*, p. 82.

41. Jawaharlal Nehru, *Jawaharlal Nehru's Speeches*, Vol. II, Publications Division, Ministry of Information and Broadcasting, New Delhi: Government of India, 1954, p. 94.

42. S. Gopal (ed.), *Selected Works of Jawaharlal Nehru*, Vol. 4 (New Series), Delhi: Oxford University Press, 1986, p. 566.

43. Nehru, *Jawaharlal Nehru's Speeches*, p. 84.

44. Nehru, *The Discovery of India*, pp. 534–35.

45. E. Zelliot, 'The Meanings of Ambedkar', Ghanshyam Shah

(ed.), *Dalit Identity and Politics*, New Delhi: Sage Publications, 2001, p. 1.

46. B. R. Ambedkar, 'Untouchables or the Children of India's Ghetto', *Dr Babasaheb Ambedkar Writings and Speeches*, Vasant Moon (ed.), Volume 5, Bombay: Government of Maharashtra, 1989, p. 19.

47. B. R. Ambedkar, *Dr Babasaheb Ambedkar Writings and Speeches*, Volume 7, Vasant Moon (ed.), Bombay: Government of Maharashtra, 1979, p. 266.

48. B. R. Ambedkar, *Dr Babasaheb Ambedkar Writings and Speeches*, Volume 7, Vasant Moon (ed.), Bombay: Government of Maharashtra, 1979, p. 198.

49. B. R. Ambedkar, 'Draft Constitution – Discussion', *Dr Babasaheb Ambedkar Writings and Speeches*, Vasant Moon (ed.), Volume 13, Bombay: Government of Maharashtra, 1994, p. 62.

50. Ambedkar, 'Untouchables or the Children of India's Ghetto', p. 19.

51. Ibid., p. 19.

52. Ibid., p. 22.

53. Ibid., p. 23.

54. Ibid., p. 24.

55. Ibid., pp. 25–26.

56. Ibid., p. 104.

57. Ibid., p. 193.

THE RAT'S GUIDE

This excerpt is taken from *A Matter of Rats: A Short Biography of Patna* by Amitava Kumar, published by Aleph Book Company in 2013.

1. Mark Jacobson, 'Big Scary Ugly Dirty Rats', *New York*, 7 November 2011, pp. 30–33.

2. Phanishwar Nath Renu, *Rinjal Dhanjal*, New Delhi: Rajkamal Prakashan, 1977, pp. 29–30.

'OH, THAT HOUSE? IT'S IN THE SEA NOW— THERE!'

This investigative article by Rahul M. was first published in the People's Archive of Rural India (PARI).

DESPOTS, DISTILLERS, POETS, AND ARTISTS: CHARACTERS OF THE COUNTRYSIDE

This excerpt is taken from *Everyone Loves a Good Drought: Stories from India's Poorest Districts* by P. Sainath.

NOTES ON THE AUTHORS

Ruskin Bond (born 1934) has been writing for over sixty years, and now has over 120 titles in print—novels, collections of stories, poetry, essays, anthologies, and books for children. His first novel, *The Room on the Roof*, received the prestigious John Llewellyn Rhys award in 1957. He has also received the Padma Shri, and two awards from the Sahitya Akademi—one for his short stories and another for his writing for children. In 2012, the Delhi government awarded him its Lifetime Achievement Award.

Vijaydan Detha (1926–2013), also known as Bijji and 'the Shakespeare of Rajasthan', has more than 800 short stories to his credit, including *Bataan ri Phulwadi* (A Garden of Tales), a fourteen-volume collection of stories that draws on folklore and the spoken dialects of Rajasthan. His stories and novels have been adapted for many plays and movies including Habib Tanvir's *Charandas Chor*, Amol Palekar's *Paheli*, and *Duvidha* by Mani Kaul. He was co-founder of Rupayan Sansthan, an institute that documents Rajasthani folklore, arts, and music; he was a recipient of the Padma Shri and Sahitya Akademi awards.

Mahasweta Devi (1926–2016) was born in Dhaka. She was educated at Vishva-Bharati and Calcutta University. She then became a writer, journalist, and professor. Her first book,

Jhansir Rani, was published in 1956. She retired from her professorship in 1984 and became a full-time writer of fiction and a champion of Adivasi rights. For her achievements as a writer and human rights worker, she has been given several awards and honours, among them the Ramon Magsaysay Award and the Jnanpith Award. Her works *Rudaali* and *Hajar Churashir Maa* have been adapted into films.

Mohandas Karamchand Gandhi (1869–1948), revered freedom fighter and civil rights activist, launched *Harijan*, a weekly magazine, in 1933 to raise awareness against the oppressive structures of caste plaguing Indian society. Alongside deliberations on economic and political matters of the time, the magazine published poetry and articles espousing ideas of social equality and enabling access to education for students from all social backgrounds. A popular feature was the 'Question Box', where M. K. Gandhi responded to questions about contemporary issues. Rabindranath Tagore and Charles Freer Andrews were frequent contributors.

Surinder S. Jodhka (born 1960) is a Professor of Sociology at Jawaharlal Nehru University, New Delhi. He has extensively researched and published on the dynamics of caste in present times, aspects of the agrarian economy, changing patterns of social and political life in contemporary rural India, and the sociology of community identities. He is the editor of the Routledge India book series on 'Religion and Citizenship' and co-editor of the Oxford University Press book series on 'Exploring India's Elite'. He is a recipient of the ICSSR Amartya Sen Award for Distinguished Social Scientists.

Amitava Kumar (born 1963) is the author of *A Matter of Rats: A Short Biography of Patna; Home Products*, which was shortlisted for the Crossword Prize; and *A Foreigner Carrying in the Crook of His Arm a Tiny Bomb,* which the *New York Times* described as a 'perceptive and soulful…meditation on the global war on terror and its cultural and human repercussions', and received the Page Turner Award. Kumar's writing has appeared in *Caravan, Harper's, The Guardian, New Yorker, Vanity Fair,* and the *New York Times*. His essay 'Pyre', first published in *Granta*, was selected by Jonathan Franzen for Best American Essays 2016. He was awarded a Guggenheim Fellowship in 2016. Kumar is Professor of English at Vassar College.

Rahul M. is a freelance journalist based out of Andhra Pradesh. He splits his time between rural reporting and investigative reporting.

Damodar Mauzo (born 1944) is a short story writer, novelist, critic, and scriptwriter who lives in Goa and writes in Konkani. He received India's highest literary honour, the Jnanpith Award, in 2022. His most recent published book is *The Wait: And Other Stories*. He was awarded the Sahitya Akademi Award in 1983, for his novel *Karmelin*, and the Vimala V. Pai Vishwa Konkani Sahitya Puraskar in 2011, for his novel *Tsunami Simon*. His collection of short stories, *Teresa's Man and Other Stories from Goa*, was nominated for the Frank O'Connor International Short Story Award in 2015. He has served as a member of the executive board of the Sahitya Akademi, New Delhi.

P. Sainath (born 1957) is a celebrated journalist noted for his groundbreaking reportage on issues such as poverty, famine, hunger, and caste discrimination. He is author of the bestselling *Everyone Loves a Good Drought: Stories from India's Poorest Districts* and has received several prestigious awards for his work including the Ramon Magsaysay Award, the Harry Chapin Media Award, the United Nations's Food and Agricultural Organisation's A. H. Boerma Prize, and the European Commission's Lorenzo Natali Prize. In 2014, he founded the People's Rural Archive of India, a multimedia platform for rural journalism.

O. V. Vijayan (1930–2005) was a pioneering author from Palakkad, best-known for writing one of the most popular Malayalam novels, a masterclass in magical realism, and a turning point in modern literature, *Khasakkinte Itihasam*. He received the inaugural Muttathu Varkey Award in 1982, and in 2003, was conferred the Padma Bhushan by the Government of India. Other significant works by Vijayan include *Gurusagaram, Madhuram Gayathi*, and *Thalamurakal*. His political cartoons and commentary have appeared in the *Statesman* and the *Hindu*.

NOTES ON THE TRANSLATORS

Ipsita Chanda is a professor at the Department of Comparative Literature and English at Foreign Languages University, Hyderabad. She has extensively contributed to several journals and books, including the edited volume *Shaping the Discourse: Women's Writings in Bengali Periodicals, 1865–1947* (2014) and *Packaging Freedom: Feminism and Popular Culture* (2003). In 2017, she wrote *Selfing the City: Single Women Migrants and Their Lives in Kolkata.*

Xavier Cota has worked as a teacher, banker, and sports administrator, and translates fiction from Konkani to English and non-fiction from Portuguese to English. His translated fiction and other articles have appeared in publications like *The Week, Man's World, Katha Prize Stories,* and Sahitya Akademi's journal. He has won the 2005 Katha Award for Translation. His Konkani-to-English translations of Damodar Mauzo's works include the short story collections *The Wait: And Other Stories, These Are My Children,* and *Teresa's Man and Other Stories from Goa,* and the novel *Tsunami Simon.* He lives in Betalbatim, Goa.

Kailash Kabir is an award-winning translator and poet of Hindi and Rajasthani who makes his home in Jodhpur, India.

Christi A. Merrill is an assistant professor of South Asian Literature and postcolonial studies at the University of

215

Michigan. Her translations from Hindi, French, and Rajasthani and essays on translation have appeared in journals such as *Genre*, *Studies in Twentieth Century Literature*, *The Iowa Review*, *Modern Poetry in Translation*, and *Indian Literature*, the Sahitya Akademi's bi-monthly journal.

A. J. Thomas is a poet, editor, and translator who writes in English. He has more than twenty books to his credit and is the former editor of Indian Literature, the Sahitya Akademi's bi-monthly journal. Thomas has taught English at Benghazi University, Libya, and worked as a Senior Consultant at IGNOU. He is a recipient of the Katha Award, AKMG Prize, and the Vodafone Crossword Award for Translation. Thomas holds a Senior Fellowship, Government of India, and was an Honorary Fellow, Department of Culture, Government of South Korea.